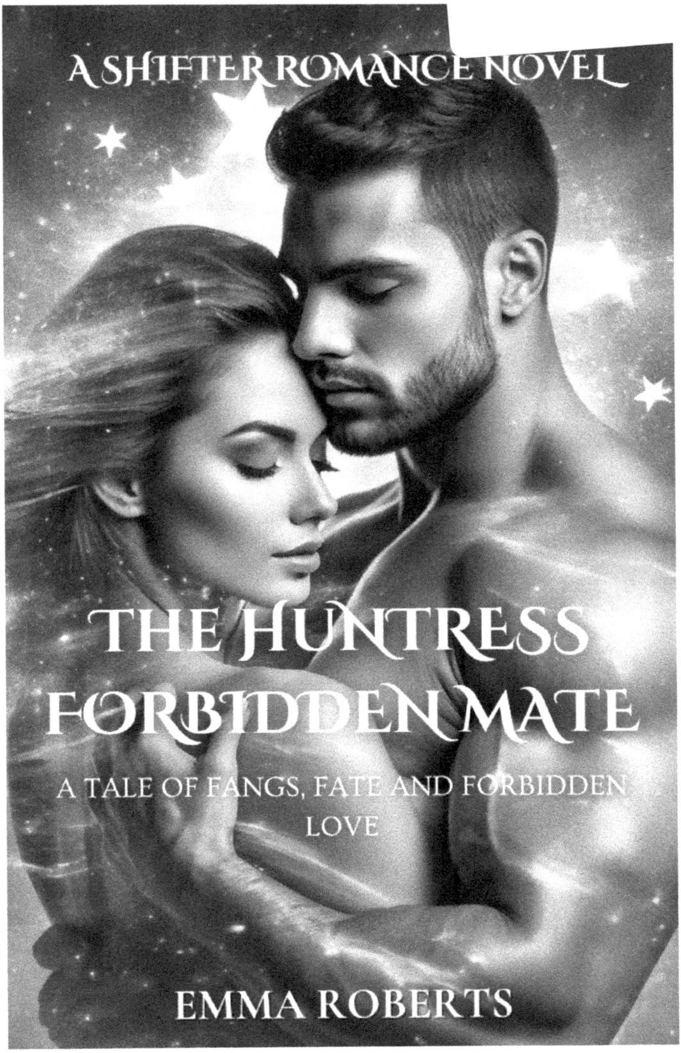

THE HUNTRESS FORBIDDEN MATE

A TALE OF FANGS, FATE AND FORBIDDEN LOVE

Copyright © 2024 by Emma Roberts

All rights reserved. This book cannot be duplicated, saved, or sent in any way—electronic, mechanical, photocopying, recording, scanning, or otherwise—without the publisher's express written consent. This book cannot be duplicated, uploaded to a website, or distributed in any other way without permission.

This book is completely fictitious. All the names, characters, and occurrences depicted in it were created by the author. Any resemblance to real people, dead or alive, places, or things is purely coincidental.

Emma Roberts asserts a moral right to be identified as the author of this work.

First edition

TABLE OF CONTENT

TABLE OF CONTENT 3
CHAPTER ONE 5
CHAPTER TWO 9
CHAPTER THREE 13
CHAPTER FOUR 20
CHAPTER FIVE 28
CHAPTER SIX 34
CHAPTER SEVEN 42
CHAPTER EIGHT 50
CHAPTER NINE 57
CHAPTER TEN 67
CHAPTER ELEVEN 75
CHAPTER TWELVE 83
CHAPTER THIRTEEN 91
CHAPTER FOURTEEN 98
CHAPTER FIFTEEN 107
CHAPTER SIXTEEN 114
CHAPTER SEVENTEEN 120
CHAPTER EIGHTEEN 129
CHAPTER NINETEEN 135
CHAPTER TWENTY 140
CHAPTER TWENTY-ONE 146
CHAPTER TWENTY-TWO 152
CHAPTER TWENTY-THREE 157
CHAPTER TWENTY-FOUR 162
CHAPTER TWENTY-FIVE 169
CHAPTER TWENTY-SIX 175
CHAPTER TWENTY-SEVEN 181

CHAPTER TWENTY-EIGHT	189
CHAPTER TWENTY-NINE	196
CHAPTER THIRTY	202
EPILOGUE	209
ABOUT THE AUTHOR	214
AUTHOR'S NOTE	216
ADDITIONAL RESOURCES	217

CHAPTER ONE

~Athena~

Three rogue wolves, all hulking figures in their shifted forms, closed in on me. I was completely out of arrows, nothing left but my trusty bow. You might think I'd be scared, but I'd face worse.

A few yards ahead, a glint of metal caught my eye. My dagger and staff! The rogues must have cut my belt and holsters off during the fight. Growls and snarls filled the air as they circled me.

"You think I'm scared of you? I'm not!" I yelled though a part of me knew it wasn't entirely true.

One of the wolves lunged. I dodged at the last second, a desperate leap bringing me within reach of my fallen weapons. Rolling to my feet, I grasped my staff in my left hand and the dagger in my right.

The rogues' bravado faltered for a moment, but they quickly recovered. Another charged, only to meet a solid blow from my staff followed by the swift plunge of my silver, wolfsbane-laced dagger into its heart. It died instantly.

The remaining two rogues couldn't hide their fear any longer. Whines replaced growls as they backed away. Aiming, I hurled my dagger. It found its mark, piercing the heart of the second wolf.

The last one, a she-wolf with glowing red eyes that spoke of her evil nature, looked utterly terrified. My staff, however, held a secret weapon. With a press of a button, a gleaming silver blade extended from its tip.

The rogue didn't stand a chance. A single thrust, a pained howl, and then silence. I deactivated the blade and retrieved my weapons from the fallen foes. Bow in one hand, staff and dagger in the other, I delivered my calling card.

A clean "R" carved into each of their foreheads with my dagger, a symbol of fear for rogue wolves everywhere. Now, introductions.

Meet Athena King, nineteen years old, with long, raven hair and piercing green eyes. There's one more detail: I hunt werewolves. But only the rogues, the outcasts banished from their packs. Not all rogues are bad, I know that. The giveaway is their eyes – gold for good, red for the likes of those I just dealt with. The problem is, that most wolves are too quick to kill before checking.

The good rogues I've met were driven out by ruthless Alphas, who beat them simply for being Omegas (low-ranking pack members). Speaking of Alphas, they're the ones I despise the most.

To the werewolf world, I'm known as Robin Hood. Cheesy, I admit, but unlike the legend, I never reveal my face. A black mask keeps my identity a secret.

Before I knew it, I was back at the familiar farmhouse. My grandparents, my only family since my parents were killed by werewolves when I was just a baby, were there. The gold coin they gave me, a constant reminder of them, hung around my neck even during hunts.

"Hey Grandma," I greeted, placing my bow on the kitchen counter. A playful scold came in reply about weapons at the table. With apologies, I moved the bow and inquired about Midnight, my Rottweiler companion.

Her excited bark from upstairs told me she was waiting. A quick hello, a flurry of greeting licks – her barks were my code: one for yes, two for no, and a disgruntled three for when I stepped on her tail. Her black fur, with distinctive brown markings, made her a beauty.

A glance in the mirror revealed my usual hunting attire – black army pants, combat boots, a leather jacket, and gloves. The mask, of course, covered my face from forehead to nose. Hunting required masking my scent, so I used a cheap yet effective perfume.

A cold shower washed away the sweat and grime of the fight. Back in my room, I changed into comfortable clothes and headed downstairs, Midnight at my heels.

My grandparents were engrossed in files. Turns out, my next mission was far away – Canada. A pack there was overrun by rogues, and they needed my help. Canada? A week from now? While a part of me worried about the distance, another reminded me I could make my arrows if needed.

"Great," I sighed, resigned. "Just until the rogue problem is under control, right?"

"Exactly," my grandpa confirmed.

A sigh escaped my lips. No choice, then. "Here's the file," Grandpa said, handing me a pale yellow folder. "You leave in a week."

The file contained pictures – the Alpha, his wolf form, the Beta, and the Third in Command. The Alpha, Hayden Lockheart, had mismatched brown and blue eyes and a completely brown wolf with black ears. Unmated, and undeniably handsome – top three Alpha material, I had to admit. But this Alpha had a reputation – a hunter-killer.

Packing commenced. A week till Canada. Here's hoping our paths don't cross.

CHAPTER TWO

~Athena~

The week flew by in a blur. The only silver lining? Midnight by my side on this adventure.

"Athena, everything's loaded in your truck. Time to hit the road," Grandma's voice snapped me from my thoughts.

"Coming," I mumbled, following Midnight's excited pace to my trusty black Ford. Thankfully, she's a dream off-leash.

A group hug with my grandparents tightened the knot of worry in my stomach. "I'll miss you guys," I choked out.

"We'll miss you too, honey. But this is a chance to make some new friends," Grandma said with a hopeful smile.

"No promises," I warned. Socializing wasn't my forte. No friends meant no targets for wolves seeking revenge. Just another layer of protection for the people I aimed to keep safe.

With a sigh, I opened the passenger door for Midnight's eager leap. "Before you go," Grandpa said, his voice serious, "promise us you'll at least try to make one friend. You can't be a lone wolf forever."

"You know why I can't," I argued, frustration bubbling up.

His hand gripped my shoulder. "Athena, promise us."

A defeated sigh escaped my lips. "Fine, one friend. You happy now?"

Beaming, they said in unison, "Much better. Here are your glasses." Grandma handed them over. "For public appearances and scent masking, remember?"

I slid them on, thanking them with another hug. Pulling away, I climbed into the driver's seat, rolling down the window for Midnight's breeze-sniffing pleasure. Her goodbye bark echoed as we pulled away.

The radio was on, random songs filled the air. After a few hours, my furry companion drifted off to sleep. Her curled-up form was undeniably adorable, but the road demanded my attention.

Long hours, gas station stops, and the occasional intoxicated encounter marked the journey. Finally, my new home in the woods emerged, complete with a master bedroom and guest rooms – comfortable and secluded.

Midnight stirred upon seeing the house, her tail wagging furiously. Once parked, I opened the door to her excited greeting. Inside, she sniffed around, a curious explorer. The house, a former vacation haven, came fully furnished.

Leaving Midnight to explore, I unloaded the boxes from my truck. After some well-deserved Netflix on my laptop, with Midnight snuggled beside me, a different kind of adventure unfolded.

Her insistent tug pulled me from the screen and into the kitchen. Leash in mouth, she conveyed a clear message: "Walk time!"

Hooking the leash onto her red collar, phone, and keys in hand, we ventured outside. Midnight led the way, her destination unknown but trusted.

The small park that came into view held families enjoying the playground. My brow furrowed in confusion. "Why are we here?" I whispered.

Ignoring me, she kept pulling, leash taut. With a resigned sigh, I unhooked her leash, letting her run free. She stopped, planting herself in front of a specific family.

"Midnight!" I called, but she wouldn't budge. Rushing towards them, I apologized for any disruption caused by my curious canine.

Then, a flicker – the woman's eyes briefly changed color. Werewolves.

"No worries, dear. New in the neighborhood?" she inquired sweetly.

I nodded, her intentions unclear.

"Well, keep an eye out for wild dogs around here," the husband warned playfully. "Best to stay in at night."

Their words were a coded message – a warning about the rogues.

"Thanks for the heads-up," I offered. "Would you be able to tell me exactly where I can find these wild dogs?"

"South and east of here," the woman replied. "Be careful."

A mental note was made – rogues, south and east. "Thank you," I muttered, walking away.

Out of sight, I crouched to Midnight's level. "Good girl," I praised, rewarding her with a high-five (or should I say, a high-four).

Back at the house, glasses cast aside, I retrieved the weapon boxes. The kitchen became my sharpening haven, Midnight adding a sentimental touch with a picture frame in her mouth. It held a painting of my grandparents on their wedding day.

"Fine, fine," I conceded, letting out a breath. "New friend, huh? Maybe after I clear out some rogues tomorrow."

A confirmatory bark, four sharp yips. With a smile, I prepped my gear for the coming day. The silence was broken by my ringing phone.

"Hello?"

"Hi sweetie," Grandma's voice flooded my ear. "Did you find the rogues?"

"Yep, south and east. Getting ready to head out tomorrow."

"Excellent! And remember you said you'd make some friends." She reminded.

"Alright, a promise is a promise. I'll go mingling after."

"OK. We love you. Take care."

"Bye."

I hung up and got ready for bed.

CHAPTER THREE

~Athena~

Midnight's tail swatted me across the face, waking me with a groan. Ignoring her sleepy readjustment, I lumbered through my morning routine.

Black army pants, combat boots, a hooded leather jacket, and gloves – the usual attire. My long black hair got wrangled into a side braid that snaked down my chest from underneath the hood. Comfortable enough, surprisingly.

Arrows filled my quiver, holsters strapped across my waist and thigh. The dagger on my thigh, staff secured at my waist. To mask my scent, half a bottle of perfume later (worth it).

Midnight's food and water bowls were refilled, and I donned my mask and hood before setting off south. Deep within the woods, I took to the trees. A clearing revealed three male rogues huddled together, their conversation muffled.

"Midnight Fire Pack it is, then. Back to the Rogue King with the news!" declared the blond one.

Before they could budge, an arrow pierced his heart, courtesy of me perched in the nearby tree. All eyes snapped in my direction as I gracefully descended. Growls of disgust rumbled from their throats.

Another arrow nocked, aimed. "Don't move a muscle, or it'll be through your eye," I threatened.

"Robin Hood, huh?" The black-haired rogue smirked. "Heard rumors about your arrival."

What?! How were they tipped off?

"How'd you—" I started but the red-haired one cut me off.

"Know? Let's just say someone squealed." His smirk widened.

Fury surged through me. "Fine. You die then."

The arrow found its mark, lodging in his chest.

Panic flickered in the remaining rogue's eyes as he bolted. An arrow found its mark, embedding itself in his fleeing form.

"I warned you," I smirked down at the corpse.

A guttural growl echoed behind me. My hand instinctively reached for another arrow, string pulled taut as I spun around.

A dark brown wolf with black ears stood its ground – Alpha Hayden.

Uh oh. Looks like I wandered a little too close to his territory. Taking a deep breath, I calmed my racing heart and steadied my breathing. Fear wasn't an option.

"Alpha Hayden. Shift!" I commanded.

Surprise flickered across his features as he acknowledged my identity. He vanished behind a tree, emerging moments later clad only in jeans.

Must. Not. Stare. At. His. Chest.

"Princess," he drawled, "surrender, and I can offer a swift demise."

"Princess? Hardly. And who said I go down easily? Besides, those jeans are doing your circulation no favors." I retorted.

"Then your death will be slow and agonizing," he growled, lunging at me.

I dodged with ease, nocking and losing an arrow in one fluid motion.

The arrow found its mark, piercing straight through his hand. A guttural groan escaped his lips as agony contorted his features.

"I could easily end you right now, Alpha," I declared, "but respect for your position stays your execution."

He ripped the arrow out, another pained groan escaping him. His eyes burned with anger. "That coin you carry… quite the charm, wouldn't you say?"

I glanced down, dread washing over me.

Oops. Back into the jacket pocket, it went. Not-so-subtle detail.

"Don't even think about it." Another arrow nocked, string pulled back.

"So it holds meaning, then?" he pressed.

A stoic silence was my only response.

He growled again, tackling me to the ground. The arrow fired in the process, finding purchase in a nearby tree.

His hands tightened around my throat. Panic surged, but adrenaline-fueled a desperate kick aimed at a very vulnerable area.

He roared in pain, rolling off me as he clutched his groin.

Seizing the opportunity, I scrambled to my feet and sent an arrow flying, lodging itself in his leg.

"One more step, and you're a dead man," I threatened, leaving my mark on the fallen rogues before disappearing into the woods.

A few well-placed loops and turns later, I confirmed I was alone. Relief washed over me as I retraced my steps back home.

The moment I entered, I made a beeline for my room. Midnight lay sprawled on the bed, surrounded by a pile of clothes. She perked up at the sound of the door opening, her gaze fixated on me.

"Did you pick out an outfit for me?" I ask her.

She barked once.

I took the pile of clothes and changed in the bathroom.

Midnight has good taste.

It was black skinny jeans with a white top and a leather jacket.

I don't even know how she got these from my closet.

I came out and Midnight had one of my black and white Converse in her mouth along with my fake glasses next to it.

I took them from her and slid on my shoes and glasses as I undid my braid and let my, now wavy, hair flow.

"Thanks, Midnight." I patted her head.

I looked down at my neck to glance at my gold coin but it was gone.

I panicked.

That asshole of an alpha must have unhooked it when he had his hands around my neck.

It must have fallen on the floor as I kicked him.

I've got to find him.

"Bye Midnight. I'll be back in a jiffy".

She barked four times before I left.//
I grabbed my keys and wallet and hopped in my truck.
I kept driving until I was in town.
There were a lot of shops and diners.
This place is huge! Finding him seems like an impossible task.
Then, by sheer coincidence, I saw him and his beta and third-in-command along with two girls in a booth through a diner window.
What are the chances!?
Pretty high.
I parked my truck in the parking lot next to the diner and made my way inside.
A waitress came up to me. "Hi, honey. You can take a seat anywhere and I'll take your order in a bit." She had a bit of a southern accent.
I took a seat in the booth behind the one that Alpha Hayden and his buddies were sitting at.
His eyes never left me ever since I entered the diner.
The waitress came to my booth and handed me a menu.
"What can I get you, darling?" She asked
I skimmed through the menu. "I'll take, the country-fried steak with mashed potatoes and gravy."
I know I didn't come here to eat, but I'm starving.
She took the menu from me as she wrote down my order. "It won't be long, dear. I'll have it out to you in a jiffy," she said with a warm smile.
"Thank you." I thanked them as she left.

I pulled out my phone to try and distract myself from Alpha Hayden's gaze on me.

Out of the corner of my eye, I saw him get up and sit across from me.

I looked up and saw him smiling.

"Can I help you?" I asked.

"I've never seen you here before. Are you new?" He asks.

"I'm new here. Just arrived about a week ago," I lied.

I can't let anyone suspect that as soon as Robin Hood arrives, I arrive.

"Cool. Where do you live?" He asks.

"In the woods. I've heard there are a lot of wild dogs around here though. It's a bit scary." I lied.

Rogues don't scare me.

"Don't be. The woods are a nice place to live in. I live with my family in the woods. I'm Hayden Lockheart by the way." He held out his hand.

"Athena King."

I shook his hand. A wave of electricity shot up my arm. In a good way.

Oh no.

I'm not his mate, am I?

I hope not. That would be awkward.

I to a look at his neck and he had my gold coin around his neck.

That made my blood boil but I kept calm.

"That's a nice gold coin." I fake complimented.

He looked down at the coin and then back at me. "Thanks, but it's not mine."

Damn right, it's not.

stood huddled. A quick sniff confirmed my suspicions – rogues. Their conversation sent a growl rumbling through my throat.

"Midnight Fire Pack, here we come," the blonde boasted. "Time to report back to the Rogue King."

Before they could budge an inch, an arrow pierced the blonde's heart. A hunter! My annoyance flared at the sight. Hunters were about as welcome as a plague of fleas.

The remaining rogues spun around, searching for the source of the attack. Down from a tree came a figure clad in black – mask, army pants, combat boots, leather jacket, gloves, and a hood – a walking arsenal. Long black hair cascaded down her back, framing eyes that gleamed an emerald green. A faint scent of cinnamon and vanilla drifted towards me – either my mate was nearby, or someone was baking cinnamon rolls (hoping for the latter).

The huntress, nocking an arrow on her bow, issued a chilling threat, "Don't even twitch, or you'll be sporting an arrow through the eye."

To my surprise, a low purr rumbled in my chest – Jordan? Was he attracted to this… huntress?

"Easy there, wolf," I scolded him, rolling my eyes. "Pretty sure those are dirty thoughts emanating from you, not me."

Ignoring him, I focused on the unfolding scene. The black-haired rogue smirked. "Robin Hood," he drawled. "The rumors about your arrival were flying faster than a rogue on the run."

Robin Hood? The legendary outlaw? I'd heard whispers, but always assumed it was a man.

"How did you-" she started but a redhead cut her off.

"Know? Let's just say someone knows about you." He smirked.

She looked mad now.

"Then you die." She let go of the string on her bow and sent the arrow through his chest.

The last rogue looked at her in complete fear. He ran backward but, I guess Robin Hood, shot an arrow through his eye.

"I warned you." She smirked at the corpse.

Ok, that's it!

If it's one thing I hate, is cocky people.

"Looks like someone hates themself," Jordan snickered.

'Shut up.'

I growled at the huntress in front of me and walked in front of her.

She grabbed an arrow and pulled the string back but didn't let it go.

"Alpha Hayden. Shift!" She commanded.

I was surprised that she knew who I was, but obeyed.

Retreating behind a tree, I shifted back into my human form, emerging clad only in a pair of jeans.

Assuming a dominant posture, I offered a "generous" proposition. "Princess, surrender immediately and I promise a swift and painless death."

Her emerald eyes narrowed. "Princess? I wouldn't be caught dead in a tiara. And let's just say your fashion sense, particularly those tight jeans, suggests a lack of blood flow to the brain." A barb well-aimed, earning a chuckle from Jordan. Traitor.
"Then your demise will be slow and agonizing," I growled, lunging at her.
With practiced agility, she dodged my attack, sending me crashing into a tree. Winded, I turned to face her, just in time to see a glint of metal headed straight for my hand. A yelp escaped my lips as the arrow lodged itself deep into my flesh. Pain shot through my arm, making me groan and cradle the wound.
"See," Robin Hood said, her voice devoid of warmth, "I could easily end you right now. But as I said, you're an Alpha."
In a surge of anger, I ripped the arrow from my hand, the pain a searing reminder of the fight. My gaze fell upon the familiar gold coin hanging around her neck. What was it doing there?
"That's a mighty fine necklace you have," I growled, the words laced with suspicion.
Her eyes flickered to the coin and then back to me. "Don't even think about it," she warned, snatching another arrow and nocking it on her bow.
A smug smirk spread across my face. "So it has some meaning to you, then?"
She remained stoic, with a mask of indifference. Frustration bubbled within me, and I lunged. She released the arrow, but it found its mark in a nearby tree.

Reacting with primal instinct, I wrapped my hands around her throat, swiftly unclasping the necklace. Just as I contemplated delivering a finishing blow, a sharp kick connected with my groin. A guttural groan escaped my lips as I doubled over, cradling the injured area.

Threats of vengeance simmered in my mind. "If I can't have children, it's on you," I snarled.

Undeterred, she retrieved another arrow and lodged it in my leg. "Don't even consider following me," she threatened, her voice cold and unwavering. "One more step, and you're a dead man."

Before disappearing into the woods, she pulled a dagger from her sheath and carved a single, bold "R" onto the forehead of the fallen rogue.

With a wince, I removed the arrow from my leg, my strength slowly returning. A glint of gold caught my eye – the fallen coin lay forgotten on the forest floor. I scooped it up and secured it around my neck.

'Looking for a keepsake or just a reminder?' Jordan's voice echoed in my head, laced with amusement.

'I'll lure her into a trap,' I countered, a determined glint in my eyes. 'No one has ever seen her without that mask. Until now.'

'Whatever,' he grumbled. 'Can we get something to eat? I'm famished.'

'First you want a run, now you want food? Honestly, I'm too hungry to argue.'

••••

The aroma of burgers and fries filled the air as I sat in Dina's Diner with Xavier, Robert, and their mates Summer and Jamie, all catching up. While waiting for our food, I recounted the encounter with the Huntress, emphasizing the stolen coin.

Xavier's question, "Was she hot?" was cut short by a sharp rap on the head from Summer.

"Just a question, woman!" he whined, rubbing his scalp.

"She wore a mask," I explained, "so I couldn't see her face. The rogues called her Robin Hood."

"I've heard whispers about her," Jamie chimed in. "She's ruthless with rogues, but some rumors suggest she's even saved a few."

Just as I was about to elaborate, a wave of cinnamon and vanilla washed over me, sending a jolt through my senses. My eyes darted towards the source of the intoxicating scent.

Standing at the entrance was a vision – a young woman with cascading black waves, emerald eyes sparkling behind glasses, and a radiant smile. She was breathtaking. And undeniably human.

'Mate, mate, mate!' Jordan roared in my mind.

"Mate," I echoed aloud, my voice thick with emotion.

"Our Luna!" Summer squealed in delight.

My gaze remained fixed on the woman as she made her way to a booth across from us. Every move she made was captivating. The waitress approached and took her order. She was alone.

Seizing the opportunity, I slid into the booth opposite her. Her eyes met mine as she looked up from her phone.

"Can I help you?" she inquired, her voice as sweet as the scent that surrounded her.

"I haven't seen you around here before," I began, a charming smile playing on my lips. "New in town?"

"Just moved in a week ago," she replied.

"Cool. Where do you live?" A dumb question, I thought, mentally kicking myself.

"Out in the woods," she answered, a hint of apprehension in her voice. "I heard there are wild dogs in the area. It's a little unsettling."

'Don't worry, beautiful,' I vowed silently. 'I'll protect you from anything.'

"The woods are a great place to live," I reassured her. "My family and I have a place out there. By the way, I'm Hayden Lockheart."

"Athena King." She shook my hand.

Sparks and tingles shot up my arm. But damn! Her name is like music to my ears.

"That's a nice gold coin." She compliments.

I looked down at the coin and then back at her. "Thanks, but it's not mine."

"Then who's is it?" She asked.

Oh no.

Gotta think of something quick.

"A friend of mine. We were walking and she dropped it when we parted ways. I found it I kept it with me so I wouldn't lose it. I have to give it back."

I lied.

The waitress came to the booth and placed a plate of food in front of her.
"Thank you." She thanked them as she dug into her food.
She moaned.
I could feel my eyes turn black and then back to normal.
My wolf purred at the sound of her moaning.
"Well, I should be heading back. Family stuff, you know? But listen, I'd hate to lose touch entirely. Athena, was it? Maybe I could have your number to keep in touch?"
She's probably going to say no.
She probably thinks I'm a creep.
"Yeah, sure." She wrote it on a napkin and handed it to me.
I winked at her before leaving with everybody else.
'Xavier, Robert. My mate is human and I know she's not going to come with me willingly. So when we see her again we are going to kidnap her. But don't tell Gena and Jamie. They'll never approve.' I explained through our link.
"Sure, Alpha. But how exactly are we supposed to locate her?" Robert asked.
'Just leave that to me. I'm going to follow her in wolf form.' I said.
They replied with a yes alpha.
I shifted into my wolf and hopped into the back of my mate's truck as she hopped in the driver's seat.

CHAPTER FIVE

~Hayden~

My mate pulled up in the driveway of a house.
That must be her place.
I heard the car door open but not the house door.
I looked around but didn't see her anywhere.
Where'd she go?
All of a sudden, she popped up right in front of me.
"Gotcha!" she yelled.
She scared the fur off me.
So much so that I fell right on my backside.
"How'd you get in here?" she asked.
I couldn't answer, still stuck in wolf form.
She rolled her eyes at me. "Just get out of my truck and leave."
Does she want me to leave already!?
She crossed her arms. "I mean now. Not next Tuesday."
I whimpered a little but did what she said. I hopped out of her truck and trotted off into the woods.
As soon as I was out of sight, I hid behind a tree and waited a bit until I knew she was inside.
Then I snuck back to her house. I saw her in her room.
She was in bed with a laptop and a dog?
Guess she has a dog now.
Looks kinda like a rottweiler.
I froze in my tracks when I saw her getting up and changing clothes.
She's so beautiful.

I know, I'm a creep.

But she's my mate. I can look.

I was bummed when she shut the curtains.

'Alpha. Everything's set for the Robin Hood takedown,' one of my guard's mind linked me.

'On my way,' I responded.

I'm gonna wait in the same spot where I first saw her and try to convince her to come with me willingly.

We'll have six guards and my beta and third in command hiding in the trees in case she gets any funny ideas about attacking me.

I got back to the clearing soon after. I had some guards haul away the rogue bodies.

Don't ask where they put them.

I shifted back into a human and threw on some jeans.

Waited a few minutes before yelling out loud.

"I got your coin! Want it back? Come and get it!" I boomed at the trees using my alpha voice.

Loud enough for her to hear if she was close by.

A sound-like movement in the leaves caught my attention.

I got ready for her appearance.

The rustling got louder with each passing second.

But instead of a girl, a bunny hopped out of the bush.

"Stupid bunny," I muttered and threw a rock at it as it hopped away.

"Sounds like someone doesn't respect wildlife," a familiar voice remarked from behind.

I turned around and came face to face with a familiar huntress.

She had her usual quiver, bow, and holsters with her.

Not much use to her now.

"You one to talk," I retorted.

She rolled her eyes at me. "Just hand over the coin."

I took it off my neck. "First, tell me what the big deal is with it."

I don't know why I care. I just do.

"None of your damn business. Just give it back," she demanded.

"Fine. Here." I tossed the coin to her.

She caught it with one hand, slipped it around her neck, then shoved it inside her jacket.

"By the way, I know you have guards hiding in the trees waiting to ambush me, and I also know your beta and third in command are hiding in that tree over there." She pointed to the exact tree they were in.

I faked a smirk. "Prove it."

She smirked back. Grabbed an arrow, and shot it right at the tree.

A loud thud came from Xavier as he hit the ground with a groan.

He had an arrow sticking right out of his backside. I fought like crazy not to bust out laughing.

"Seriously!? How am I supposed to sit down with this thing in me!?" he hollered at her as he got to his feet.

"Beats me," she replied before taking off.

As she walked away, she peppered the trees with arrows right where my guards were hiding.

"This ain't my first rodeo with an ambush!" she yelled before disappearing out of sight.

I hated her with a burning passion.

'Hey! Don't talk about her like that!' My wolf snarled at me through the mind link.

'Why are you sticking up for her!? We have a mate!' I roared back.

'Don't care! Just don't badmouth her!' He shut down the link before I could argue.

What was his deal? "Those of you with unfortunate arrow wounds in your butt, proceed to the pack infirmary for immediate medical attention!" I yelled at the remaining guards before heading back to the pack house myself.

Man, that huntress could get under my skin.

••••

~Athena~

Ugh, if only I could just kill that alpha. Such a total jerk. Here I am, not even trying to steal his Luna.

Right. Forgot about the whole Mateless thing.

After that whole ambush fiasco, I went home and crashed in bed, it was getting late anyway.

Now Midnight's on me again to get out there, but honestly, I'm just too lazy and frankly, don't care.

"Midnight, I'm not going anywhere today," I declared.

She barked twice then flashed a picture of my grandparents.

"Fine. But you can't keep pulling that trick on me," I grumbled, giving in.

Threw on a red top, dark jeans, black suspenders, and my trusty Converse.

A quick pit stop to fill Midnight's bowl before heading out.

Decided to walk instead of driving, let's face it, I was starting to feel a little on the chubby side.

Wandering around town, I couldn't shake the feeling of being followed.

Turned around and spotted a black van.

Picked up the pace, weaving through the streets to see if it was sticking to me.

Yep, it was.

If some creep thought he could get fresh, he had another thing coming.

The van screeched to a halt in front of me, the window rolling down to reveal a sunglasses-wearing dude.

Alpha Hayden!? Seriously, what did he want now?

"Get in the van," he barked.

"Nope," I replied, flat as a board.

He whipped out a gun, aiming it right at my head.

"Get. In. The. Van." He repeated, slow and menacing.

"You think a little gun scares me?" I scoffed before launching a flying kick and knocking the weapon out of his hand. "Nope, not even a little bit."

All the guys piled out of the van. Recognized the other two as his beta and third-in-command, Xavier and Robert, I think.

Xavier lunged for me from behind, but I dodged him and returned the favor with a well-placed kick right where I'd tagged him with the arrow earlier.

He groaned. "Again!? Why does it always gotta be my butt!?"

"Well, no offense, but you kind of brought this on yourself," I retorted.

Suddenly, arms wrapped around me – Robert, hoisted me clean off the ground, leaving me kicking in the air.

Hayden tried to grab my legs, but I connected with his nose instead. Hard.

He cupped his nose, groaning in pain. "Get her in the van!"

Robert practically dragged me into the back of the black van.

"Let me go or you'll regret this," I threatened.

"Nice try, sweetheart," Hayden smirked. "You're coming with us."

Just my luck, the day I forget my silver dagger.

Looks like I just got kidnapped by werewolves.

CHAPTER SIX

~Athena~

The van lurched to a halt. Hayden dabbed at his nose, the blood still staining his fingers. Serves him right.

The back doors flew open, revealing Hayden. "Get out," he ordered.

"Let me go. Don't make me break your nose again," I countered, my voice laced with steel.

"Just get out. Unless you want to spend the rest of your life in this van." He smirked, but it didn't reach his eyes.

I scowled and climbed out, the vastness of the house before me momentarily stealing my breath. It was huge!

Hayden reached for my arm, but I shrugged him off. "I can walk myself," I pointed out, annoyance coloring my tone.

I followed him inside with a sigh and a curt nod. My stomach, the ultimate traitor, rumbled loudly.

"Food?" I blurted out.

Robert shot me a bewildered look. "Yes."

"Excellent." I bee-lined for the kitchen, a sense of relief washing over me as I raided the cabinets. Chips, chocolate, cinnamon rolls, pizza – a feast of junk food.

I piled it all on the counter, the stress of the situation fueling my hunger. Robert and Xavier watched me with a mix of curiosity and apprehension, while Hayden stood by, a strange smile playing on his lips.

"Stress eater!" I declared defensively, catching their stares. "Don't judge."

They averted their eyes, but Hayden's gaze remained fixed on me.

"Any other… eating… quirks?" Xavier asked awkwardly.

"Fear eater too," I replied, stuffing my face with pizza. "Can't help myself. Food just tastes better when I'm scared."

Another round of bewildered looks followed.

"What? Sue me for having taste buds!"

Hayden and Xavier seemed to lose interest, leaving me alone with Robert, his job clearly to prevent escape. They'd introduced themselves earlier, oblivious to my already knowing their names.

As Robert reached for a chip, I slapped his hand away. "Ow! No need for violence," he whined.

"Deal with it," I muttered, the sound of barking growing louder.

That bark was unmistakable. "Midnight?" I called out.

There she was, bounding into the kitchen in Hayden's arms, Xavier trailing behind. They were all sporting scratches and bite marks. Hayden's nose had finally stopped bleeding, but a red mark marred its bridge.

Midnight spotted me and launched herself into my arms. "You kidnapped her?!" I yelled, outrage mixing with relief.

"She's your twin, alright? Fiesty and violent," Xavier groaned, rubbing his arm.

"Well, you deserved it," I shot back.

Midnight, ever the opportunist, started devouring the pizza on the counter.

"Stress eater, huh?" Robert mused. "Fear eater too?"

"Nope," I replied, earning a confused nod. "She's a fear biter." I smirked, watching Robert and Xavier exchange nervous glances.

"That explains the chew toy treatment!" Xavier exclaimed.

"Much better than kidnapping, wouldn't you say?" I said sarcastically, earning a smirk from Hayden.

"Only you can turn me on with sarcasm," he purred, drawing closer.

"Pervert," I muttered, but a mischievous glint sparked in my eyes. Not going to let this escalate. Play along, then escape.

I snaked my arms around his neck, running my fingers through his hair. He visibly relaxed, leaning into my touch. Robert and Xavier wore expressions that screamed 'awkward turn.'

I leaned in, my breath tickling his ear. "Kiss me," I whispered. "See what happens."

He leaned in slowly, our breaths mingling. Just as our lips were about to touch, I kneed him square in the stomach. Before he could react, I unleashed a flurry of punches and a final blow to his back, sending him crashing to the floor.

"Why'd you do that?" Robert sputtered, bewildered.

"So I can do this." I grabbed the last chocolate bar, shoving it in my mouth. Then, with a swift kick to his stomach, followed by a powerful blow to the back of his head (a little too powerful, judging by the way he slumped), I rendered him unconscious. Xavier, ever the coward, had already made a strategic retreat. Wimp.
Hayden, slowly rising, growled at me. "You're not going anywhere."
"Yes, I am. You're in no shape to boss me around, dickhead," I retorted.
His growl deepened, interrupted by a sharp crack. He slapped me.
I stood frozen, a burning sensation on my cheek. But my defiance remained.
A slow turn of my head revealed him, regret and shame etched on his face.
"Big mistake," I growled, before launching a fist at his jaw with all my might.
He crumpled to the floor with a sickening thud, blood blooming on his lips. Snatching Midnight, who whimpered and burrowed into my arms, I sprinted towards the nearest window. With a determined shove, I crashed through the glass, leaving behind a trail of minor cuts on my arms. Setting Midnight down, I plunged into the dense forest, only to be intercepted by familiar figures. Arrows flew from my bow, pinning them to the trees.
"Luna," one of them called, voice heavy with apology, "you have to come with us."
Luna? No way. The only way that could be…

Oh god. I'm his mate?
This escape attempt just became crucial. "Not happening," I declared. "Leave, and you walk away unharmed. Stay, and missing limbs are a guarantee."
A flicker of fear crossed their faces, quickly replaced by a hardened resolve. They charged, but my reflexes were honed. A swift kick to the groin for one, a well-placed blow to the face for another. The last lunged, missing his mark completely. A final kick to the back of his head sent him sprawling unconscious.
Midnight followed at my heels as we disappeared deeper into the forest. A growl erupted from behind, raw and primal. I didn't need to turn around to know it was Hayden.
Spotting a sturdy branch overhead, I knew what I needed to do. With a burst of strength, I grabbed it and swung myself around, kicking out with my foot to send Hayden flying as I completed the arc.
My heart pounded as I raced back towards my house. I needed to warn them, not as Athena, but as Robin Hood, the elusive huntress.
Finally, Midnight and I reached the familiar sanctuary of home, exhaustion settling in. I quickly prepared Midnight's food and donned my huntress gear, leaving my loyal companion behind before transforming back into Robin Hood.
The edge of Hayden's territory came into view, guarded by two figures with disdain etched on their faces.

"What is it you want, hunter?" one of them spat, his voice dripping with hatred. This, this was why I couldn't be his mate. Acceptance would be a distant dream.

"I need to speak with your alpha. It's urgent," I replied, my voice steady.

"The alpha is busy. He's dealing with his mate, so why don't you just skulk back to wherever you came from?" I cut him off before he could finish his venomous rant.

"Tell him it's about Athena King. I'm sure you've heard the name."

Surprise flickered across their faces, followed by a moment of hesitation. Then, their eyes glazed over – mind-linking.

~Hayden~

I should have followed her. I shouldn't have let her leave. I needed my mate by my side. When I got her back, locking her up wouldn't be out of the question, even if it branded me a monster. All that mattered was having her near me.

It had only been thirty minutes, yet my office was a wreck, a mirror of the turmoil within me. The sting of my slap on her face felt like a betrayal. I deserved that punch. What was wrong with me? My wolf snarled its agreement, which I promptly ignored, wallowing in self-loathing.

'You think?' my wolf growled sarcastically.

Suddenly, a link jolted me out of my brooding. 'Alpha, there's someone here to see you. The huntress you encountered.' Not now. Why now?
'What does she want?' I growled back, frustration lacing my voice.
'She says it's about Athena King. Our Luna.'
The mention of her name was like a shot of adrenaline, instantly perking up my ears. Did she know about my mate?
'I'm on my way,' I responded, already moving towards the edge of my territory.
There, I found my guards glaring at Robin Hood with undisguised contempt. She tensed up upon seeing me.
"Leave us," I instructed the guards, their departure leaving us alone.
"What do you want?" I demanded of the huntress before me.
"I want you to stay away from Athena. Mate or not," she spat defiantly.
"Why? Why should I stay away from my mate?" My voice rose in anger.
She looked down at her bow, a silent battle raging within her. When she met my gaze again, a flicker of vulnerability danced in her multicolored eyes. Slowly, she began to remove her hood, then the mask hiding her face.
The stammered word escaped my lips, "A-Athena."
Her voice, laced with a mix of resignation and a strange protectiveness, explained, "This is why I can't be with you. But I won't reject you and leave you shattered. Just...give me some time."

With that, the familiar mask and hood returned, obscuring her features as she disappeared into the trees.

Left alone, I crumpled to my knees, tears blurring my vision. My mate, the one destined for me by fate, was everything I loathed – a hunter. They were the embodiment of the pain that had ripped my life apart.

Yet, a primal urge pulsed within me. Logic screamed rejection, but my heart ached for her touch. Despite the contradiction, I yearned to hold her close, regardless of her lineage.

Respecting her plea, though a battle raged within, I knew I had to grant her the space she requested.

CHAPTER SEVEN

~Hayden~

The last three weeks have been a nightmare. Sleep and food have been scarce. My wolf has been eerily silent. Occasionally, rogues appear with Athena's calling card, leaving me frantic with worry. She could be badly hurt, alone... I know she's strong, but she's still my mate, and it's my duty to be concerned.

Sneaking into her house, I stole a hoodie for the comfort of her scent. Leaving notes at her door expresses my desperate need for her while respecting her space. A run is what I need.

Emerging from my room, I headed outside. Stripping down, I shifted, holding my clothes in my mouth. Handing control over to Jordan, we sprinted. A fallen tree loomed ahead, but with a powerful leap, he landed flawlessly on all fours.

Suddenly, he stopped, retreating behind a tree and relinquishing control. He urged me to shift back.

Obeying, I stepped out, greeted by the intoxicating scent of my mate. As I peeked around the tree, I witnessed her deliver a swift punch and arrow to a rogue. Another one snuck up behind her, unnoticed in her focus on the first attacker. She finished him off, yet remained unaware of the approaching threat.

A growl erupted from me as I lunged at the unsuspecting rogue. Athena whirled around, ready to fire, but her arrow remained holstered upon seeing me snap the rogue's neck.

"Alpha Hayden, what are you doing here? You could have been hurt," she questioned, concern in her voice.

"You're worried about me?" I smirked.

"Never mind that," she countered, "what happens to the pack if you're hurt?"

"Not true," I corrected. "You'll lead the pack."

"The pack would never accept a huntress as their leader, nor would they trust me," she argued, turning to leave. But I grabbed her wrist, spinning her around.

"I don't care." I pulled her into a tight embrace, nuzzling her neck. "As long as I'm with you. And for hitting you, I apologize."

A gentle kiss grazed her neck, sending shivers down her spine. A triumphant smirk played on my lips.

The kisses continued, lingering on her "sweet spot," the intended marking location.

Pulling away, I whispered, "Not yet, but soon." A soft kiss landed on her forehead.

"I-I have to go. Midnight is waiting," she stammered.

"Can I join you? I couldn't bear being away any longer. I need you by my side," I pleaded.

"Just for today," she agreed, stepping away and walking off.

I followed, reaching for her hand, only to have it snatched away. Rejection stung.

My arm encircled her shoulder, but she shrugged it off. Another blow.

Undeterred, I wrapped my arm around her waist, pulling her closer. A smack to the hand sent a message loud and clear. Why wouldn't she let me touch her?

"Throw the dog a bone," I muttered in frustration.

Reaching her house, Midnight greeted me with a ferocious growl. What did I ever do to her? Besides dognapping, that is.

"Midnight, it's okay. He's just staying here for today," Athena soothed the wolf.

Midnight glared in my direction before slinking away.

"I don't think she likes me," I assumed.

"Well, you haven't exactly given her a reason to," Athena pointed out. "I'm going to shower and change. Make yourself at home."

She disappeared into a room, her scent lingering in the air, my drug.

Wandering into the living room, my eyes caught a picture of her with an elderly couple. Another photo depicted a baby held by a younger couple. The women in both pictures wore a gold coin necklace identical to Athena's. Her grandparents and parents, no doubt.

Settling on the couch with the picture of the young couple and baby, I became engrossed, only to be startled by a voice.

"What are you doing with that?" my mate inquired.

She was clad in white shorts, a black top, and blue suspenders, glasses noticeably absent.

44

"Just looking," I replied.

She gently retrieved the picture frame from my grasp and placed it back in its oriSummerl spot on the shelf.

Curiosity blooming, I inquired, "Are those your parents?"

Her body visibly tensed, and a single, strained "Yes," escaped her lips. Her gaze remained fixed on the photo, a flicker of vulnerability flickering in her eyes.

Concerned, I approached her from behind and wrapped my arms around her in a comforting embrace. Her muscles yielded slightly, a flicker of relief washing over her features.

Hoping to lighten the mood, I switched topics. "Why did you pull away when I tried to touch you back in the woods?"

She turned in my arms to face me, explaining, "Because I was disguised as Robin Hood. If the rogues knew I had someone special, they'd exploit that weakness."

A triumphant smirk played on my lips. "So, I am someone special to you, then?"

"They would have killed you," she countered, her voice laced with concern.

"Just a reminder," I pointed out, "I'm an Alpha. I believe I'm capable of defending myself."

"Being an Alpha doesn't guarantee invincibility. You need training, Hayden. It's not an inherent skill."

Hopeful, I inquired, "Can you teach me?"

She raised an eyebrow, a challenge gleaming in her eyes. "Not sure you're up to the task."

"Please," I pleaded. "There's nothing I can't handle."

A smirk returned to her face. "Follow me, then."

She led me downstairs, revealing a well-equipped basement. Punching bags, weights, jump ropes - a veritable training ground. An assortment of weapons adorned the walls.

"Don't even think about touching those," she commanded sternly.

"Why not?" I questioned, intrigued.

"Made of silver," she explained simply.

I instinctively took a step back from the weapons.

"Throw a punch at me," she instructed.

My eyes widened in disbelief. "What? Not. I wouldn't dream of hurting you."

"Consider yourself fortunate," she countered. "Very few people have ever laid a hand on me."

'Thank goodness,' I thought to myself.

"Still," I persisted, "I refuse to punch my mate."

"Just do it, you big wimp," she teased.

With a hesitant breath, I pulled my fist back, closing my eyes and bracing for impact.

But nothing happened.

Opening my eyes, I saw her hand clamped firmly around mine, stopping it just inches from her face. In a swift move, she twisted my wrist and sent me sprawling onto the mat.

"Keep your wrist straight or you'll risk a break," she instructed. "And don't be afraid to throw a real punch."

"Was the whole flipping thing really necessary?" A groan escaped my lips as I struggled to my feet, feeling the strain of the workout.

"Always strive to overpower your opponent," she explained. "It increases your probability of victory."

"I think I've had enough 'teaching' for one day," I groaned, feeling the workout.

"Weakling," she chuckled before heading upstairs.

'Great, just got my butt handed to me,' Jordan snickered in my head.

'I wasn't trying to hurt her,' I defended myself mentally.

Upstairs, I found Athena glued to her laptop. "What are you doing?" I inquired.

"I need to tell my grandparents... about you," she admitted, her voice laced with nervousness.

My nerves buzzed with a mix of excitement and apprehension. I settled down beside her as she initiated a video call.

The screen flickered to life, revealing the elderly couple from the picture frame.

"Hello, dear. Did any rogue attacks happen today?" The woman's question was laced with concern, reflected in the lines etched on her face.

"No, Grandma, I'm perfectly fine. I have some news," Athena revealed, her voice trembling slightly. I reached for her hand, offering silent comfort. My touch appeared to offer a touch of comfort, as she seemed to loosen up a bit.

"Alright, what is it?" the man prompted.

Taking a deep breath, she declared, "Please don't freak out, but it turns out I have a werewolf mate."

The woman's eyes darted to the man. "See, Hank? I told you so! Pay up!"

The man, likely Hank judging by their conversation, retrieved a rolled-up bill from his wallet and handed it to Linda with a grumble. "Not fair," he muttered.

This exchange filled in the blanks - their names were Linda and Hank.

"What's going on?" Athena asked, bewildered. "Did you two place a bet on me?"

Linda offered a blunt confirmation. "Yes. Well, more like I did. I always knew you'd find your werewolf mate eventually. Now, where's this mystery man?"

A sly smile played on Athena's lips as she glanced at me. "He's right here," she declared, placing the laptop on my lap.

"Hello," I managed, nervousness creeping into my voice.

"Alpha Hayden?" they both echoed, confused.

"How'd you know who I am?" I inquired.

"We keep files on every alpha worldwide," Athena explained. "That's how I recognized your wolf form."

"Already keeping tabs on me, are we?" I teased, a smirk forming as Athena's cheeks flushed pink.

"Hayden," Linda said sternly, "we're entrusting you with our granddaughter's safety. Don't mess this up. And use protection," she added pointedly. "Being a great-grandma isn't in the cards yet."

"Grandma!" Athena exclaimed, her cheeks burning even brighter as I chuckled.

"We can't stay any longer, dear. Goodbye, sweetheart," Hank finished, and then ended the video call.

Placing the laptop on the coffee table, Athena announced, "I'm turning in for the night. It's getting late. You're welcome to stay as long as you'd like, but you can leave whenever you feel ready."

She started to rise, but I reacted quickly, grabbing her waist and gently pulling her back onto the couch.

"Is it alright if I stay in bed with you tonight? I can barely sleep when you're not there." I pleaded

A sigh escaped her lips, but then she offered a small nod. She walked to her bedroom, removing her suspenders before climbing into bed.

I joined her, wrapping my arm around her. Her breathing gradually slowed into a peaceful rhythm, and I knew she was asleep.

"I love you," I whispered, placing a soft kiss on her forehead before drifting off to sleep myself.

CHAPTER EIGHT

~Hayden~

The coldness was starting to creep in. I huddled closer to the nearest warmth.

Suddenly, a wet sensation tickled my face. "Athena, stop it," I mumbled with a smile playing on my lips.

Cracking my eyelids, I saw Midnight showering my face with enthusiastic licks.

A groan escaped me. "Aw, dang it! Stupid dog."

Jordan's laughter echoed in my head, mocking my predicament.

Pushing Midnight gently onto the floor, I wiped away the froth with a grimace.

Always thought waking up next to your mate would be a picture of beauty. Wrong.

Athena sported a serious case of bedhead, claiming half the bed for herself. A soft snore escaped her lips, and a streak of drool decorated her cheek.

Despite it all, she still looked adorable.

'Whipped,' Jordan pointed out smugly.

'Aren't you?' I countered playfully.

A sudden jolt as Athena leaped out of bed and sprinted towards the bathroom startled me awake.

I tried to follow, but the door was locked. Sounds of retching and groans filtered through.

"Baby, you okay?" I called out worriedly.

The door creaked open a sliver. "I'm sick and on my period. Worst combo ever. Shower time." She mumbled before disappearing back into the bathroom.

Surprise breakfast, it is then. Maybe pampering would help.

I headed downstairs and started whipping up a breakfast feast, not forgetting to fill Midnight's bowl.

Cooking? No problem for this Alpha.

Just as I sizzled a strip of bacon, a sniffing sound drew my attention. "Bacon!" Athena practically materialized, her voice thick with sleep. "Gimme, gimme, gimme!"

"Aw, you ruined the surprise," I groaned, defeated.

"Chocolate and bacon? My senses become super werewolfy." She snatched a piece of bacon before I could protest.

Wrapping my arms around her from behind, I felt a familiar spark ignite. "How are you feeling?"

"Like the next time I hurl, it'll be all over you unless you let me go." She threatened though a smile played on her lips.

I held on tighter. "Risk it."

She doubled over, her face paling. More retching sounds filled the air.

This time, I relented and backed away, a helpless chuckle escaping me as she burst into laughter.

"'Risk it' my ass," she wheezed between laughs.

Pouting playfully, I muttered, "Just eat your breakfast."

The rest of the day unfolded in a movie marathon on the couch. Thankfully, the vomiting subsided, leaving just a lingering fever.

Her fevered ramblings were a bit concerning, but I knew it was just the sickness talking. She even recounted rogue-hunting adventures in faraway places.

There was a flicker of hope when she called me cute in her feverish state. But hey, a guy can dream, right?

Midway through the movie, a pair of arms snaked around my waist. While I didn't mind the sudden affection, it was uncharacteristic of her.

"Athena, what's this about?" I questioned a hint of confusion in my voice.

A dramatic sigh escaped her lips. "So you don't enjoy my company? Fine then," she sighed dramatically, pulling away with a playful pout.

'Way to go, genius,' Jordan chimed in sarcastically.

Rolling my eyes internally, I turned back to my mate. "Just asking." I sheepishly admitted, pulling her back into my embrace.

"Every time we cuddle, my fever seems to go down a bit." She revealed softly.

'She's going into heat, you goofball!' Jordan roared in my head.

Panic surged through me. Marking was necessary. But I knew she wouldn't want it forced, especially with the full moon approaching.

Why did this have to be so complicated?

'Mark her or I will,' Jordan growled menacingly.

'No way! It's her choice,' I growled back, defending my stance.

"Athena?" I asked cautiously.

"Yes?" Her voice was laced with vulnerability.

"Can I... uh... mark you?" I stammered, my cheeks burning.

She stared at me, disbelief clouding her eyes. "Jerk."

With that, she stormed off to her room, slamming the door shut and locking the knob.

Defeated, I pressed my forehead against the cool wood. "I'm sorry. Please open the door, baby. Please let me in."

"Get out of my house!" she yelled, anger lacing her words.

Letting out a defeated sigh, I obeyed.

'Nice going genius.' Jordan growled.

'Shut up. This is your fault. You wanted me to mark her or you would do it by force.' I growled back

He blocked me out.

I shifted into my wolf and started running.

••••

~Athena~

That jerk.

Only one day, and he already wants to mark me? What a massive... jerk, asshole, jackass, and even a... ugh... horny alpha!

Can't he control his urges?

Ugh! I need some fresh air.

I quickly threw on my hunting gear and bolted outside.

Deeper and deeper I went into the woods, the trees growing thicker around me.

Suddenly, a rustling sound emerged from the bushes, growing louder and more frantic.

Nocking an arrow on my bow, I held my aim steady. Just before I let loose, a familiar face emerged from the foliage.

"Stupid rose bush thorns," he grumbled, brushing them off.

The tension eased from my shoulders as I loosened my hold on the bow, lowering it carefully. "Justin?"

He looked up, a smile spreading across his face. "Robin?"

(Short for Robin Hood, a nickname he uses for me.)

I rushed forward and wrapped him in a tight hug.

Justin Wood. One of the few decent rogues I've had the pleasure of meeting. His twin sister, Beth Wood, wasn't far behind. Their wolf forms are known as Lake and Lexi.

"Where's Beth?" I asked, pulling away slightly.

A familiar voice answered from behind. "Right here."

Turning around, I saw Beth standing there, arms outstretched invitingly.

Taking her offer, I pulled her into a warm embrace.

They are both black wolves with special powers. Their alpha abused them because only he knew about them and it threatened his power as alpha. They filled me in on the details during our first encounter. I spared their lives, and our friendship blossomed in the forest. Sharing stories and laughter, we bonded deeply.

Releasing the hug from Beth, I stepped back. "What brings you guys here?"

"Alpha Mac found us," Justin explained. "We had to leave California."

"You're welcome to crash here. I've got tons of space," I offered.

"But wouldn't that mean you'd be stuck as Robin Hood the whole time?" Beth questioned.

"I trust you guys to keep my secret under wraps."

"Absolutely," Justin agreed. "You don't have to explain anything."

I nodded. "Besides, someone else already knows. My mate. Alpha Hayden."

"Man, that's rough," Justin offered with a sympathetic look.

"No worries," I brushed it off. "Let's head back. My house is just this way."

Leading them home, I finally removed the mask and hood upon entering.

"Wow, you're stunning!" Beth exclaimed.

"Thanks," I managed, a slight smile forming.

Justin stood there, speechless.

"Something on my face?" I asked playfully.

"You're beautiful," he finally admitted, a blush creeping up his neck.

A warmth spread across my cheeks, though I doubt they noticed.

"Come on, let's get you settled in your rooms."

"Wait, what's your real name?" Justin asked before I could move.

"Athena," I answered.

"The Greek goddess?" Beth chimed in, surprised.

"You know about Greek myths?" I questioned, raising an eyebrow.

"There were a lot of libraries in our old place," she explained.

I nodded in understanding.

Suddenly, Midnight came bounding towards us, barking excitedly at the newcomers.

"This is Midnight," I introduced. "Don't worry, Midnight, they're friendly rogues."

Midnight calmed down after some head scratches from Justin.

With the introductions over, I showed the twins to their rooms. Exhausted, I changed into more comfortable clothes and flopped onto my bed.

It's been a long day, and my fever feels like it's getting worse. Why on earth did Hayden want to mark me already?

CHAPTER NINE

~Athena~

The television's flickering light roused me from sleep. Ugh, the fever was still clinging on. I shuffled downstairs, finding Beth glued to the couch, channel surfing with a distant look.

"What time did you wake up?" I croaked, my voice thick.

"Couldn't catch any Zzz's," she mumbled, eyes glued to the screen.

"Anything to eat?" I offered, hoping to spark a conversation.

"Nah, I'm good," she replied without looking away.

An uneasy feeling settled in my gut. Beth had been acting like a different person lately, withdrawn and quiet. Pancakes seemed like a good distraction, so I started mixing the batter.

Footsteps thumped down the stairs. Justin appeared, rubbing the sleep from his eyes.

I slapped a pancake on a plate and slid it towards him. "Here you go, sleepyhead."

He devoured it gratefully. "Something wrong with Beth? She's been acting all distant."

Justin let out a heavy sigh, his appetite disappearing. "Guess what? Beth met her mate yesterday, right before we picked you up."

"Oh no!" I exclaimed, then caught myself. "Wait, isn't that a good thing?"

He shook his head, his expression grim. "Rejected her."

My blood ran cold. "Tell me his name," I growled, a dark glint flickering in my eyes. "And I'll turn him into a pincushion."

"No! Beth doesn't want to talk about it, and she begged me not to tell you. Please, don't do anything rash," Justin pleaded.

Gritting my teeth, I forced myself to calm down. "Fine. I won't say a word to her. But the moment I see that jerk, an arrow's finding a new home in his anatomy."

"I'll let you know when that happens," Justin conceded. "But right now, we need to get her mind off things."

A mischievous grin spread across my face. "I have an idea, but we must wait until nightfall."

"Why the wait?" he asked, raising an eyebrow.

"Just trust me," I smirked.

"That glint in your eyes… it's kinda scary," he chuckled nervously.

"Just a bit of my natural charisma," I said with a wink, sliding another pancake onto his plate. "Take this to Beth. Even if she says no, I don't believe her for a second."

He took the plate and headed back to the living room.

The thermometer under my tongue confirmed my suspicions — 103.1. This fever needed to go, fast. Maybe a cold shower would do the trick. I shut off the stove and retreated upstairs.

After a refreshing shower and some teeth-brushing, I rejoined the others downstairs. Beth sat alone in the kitchen, while Justin occupied the couch. Still a few hours until sunset.

"Hey Beth, up for an outing or something?" I asked tentatively.

She gave a small shake of her head. "No thanks, not really in the mood today."

"How about pizza and a movie marathon?" I suggested, hoping to tempt her.

A flicker of interest sparked in her eyes. "That sounds good actually." She pushed herself off the counter and headed towards the living room.

I whipped out my phone and ordered a feast – a large pepperoni and a three-meat pizza. They arrived within twenty minutes, and Justin beat me to the door.

The pizza delivery guy took one whiff of Justin and inhaled deeply. "Mate," he muttered under his breath.

Hold on a minute... Justin's gay? Well, that changes things. Supportive best friend mode: activate!

I grabbed the pizzas and paid the delivery guy, then playfully shoved Justin out the door and shut it behind him.

Placing the pizzas on the counter, I peeked out the window. There they were, locked in a kiss on the porch.

Aww, how sweet! Mental note: a major teasing session for Justin later.

Bursting with excitement, I raced into the living room and squealed, collapsing onto the couch next to Beth. "Justin found his mate!"

A genuine smile spread across Beth's face. "He did? That's amazing, I'm so happy for him!"
Relief washed over me. Happy for her brother, even if her own heart was hurting.
The door creaked open, swinging inwards to reveal Justin alongside a stranger balancing a pizza box.
"Everyone, meet Johnny," Justin announced with a grin, gesturing towards his companion. "Johnny, this is my sister Beth and my best friend Athena."
Johnny's gaze darted around the room, landing on me with a jolt. "Wait a minute," he blurted, finger pointed in my direction, "she's human?"
A nonchalant shrug escaped my shoulders. "Having a werewolf mate isn't exactly a standard issue," I explained. "But I'm familiar with your kind."
A moment of processing passed across Johnny's face before he offered a sheepish nod. "Okay, sorry about that."
"No worries," I waved him off, already reaching for another plate.
Sensing a potential awkwardness, Justin spoke up. "So, you guys are cool with, uh, me being gay?"
Before he could finish, Beth shot up from the couch and pulled him into a warm embrace. Mirroring her action, I squeezed him tightly. "We support you fully, Justin," I declared.
We spent a decent chunk of time getting to know Johnny. It turned out his parents kicked him out after discovering his sexuality, forcing him to take a job delivering pizzas. Fortunately, he had a small apartment nearby, and Justin was already considering moving in with him.

One detail I couldn't miss – Johnny's eyes held the telltale glint of a rogue. But after a quick check, I concluded he wasn't a threat. Just another lost soul trying to navigate the world.

The rest of the afternoon melted away in a haze of pizza and movie marathons. As twilight painted the sky in hues of orange and purple, I decided it was time to enact my grand plan.

With a flourish, I stood and began drawing the curtains shut, shrouding the room in a comforting darkness. Candlelight flickered to life as I lit several scattered around the room, casting an inviting glow.

"What's going on, Athena? And what's the deal with the candles?" Beth inquired, her voice laced with curiosity.

"Just hold on a sec," I replied mysteriously, disappearing into the basement for a brief moment.

I returned with a familiar wooden board emblazoned with cryptic letters and symbols – an Ouija board.

Justin's jaw dropped. "An Ouija board!? Seriously, Athena, that's your plan?"

I flashed him a confident grin and winked. "Come on, at least give it a shot. It might be fun!"

"Where'd you even get that?" Beth questioned, eyeing the board with a mix of amusement and apprehension.

"My mom's," I explained. "Grandma told me stories about how she and her friends used to play with it, and supposedly it worked."

We all settled down on the floor, the Ouija board forming a mysterious centerpiece between us. My fingers and theirs hovered lightly over the planchette, a strange anticipation hanging heavy in the air.

"Alright, so what do we ask it?" I inquired, breaking the silence.

Beth, a mischievous glint in her eyes, piped up, "Is Justin a total idiot?" before erupting in laughter.

"Hey!" Justin protested good-naturedly.

Much to our amusement, the planchette began to move, gliding steadily across the board until it landed firmly on "yes." Beth and I burst into another fit of giggles, barely managing to keep our fingers on the tool.

"Looks like I can't catch a break even from the spirit world," Justin muttered, a hint of mock defeat in his voice.

"Alright, my turn," I declared. "Can you give us any indication you're present?"

Two seconds ticked by, then a crash erupted from the kitchen, shattering the tense silence. We all whipped our heads around in unison, eyes darting towards the source of the sound. I turned back to the Ouija board.

"Okay, that's a sign, we get it," I addressed the unseen entity. "But something a little less... dramatic next time, alright?"

My gaze scanned the kitchen counter, where one of the stools now lay sprawled on the floor, overturned by the unseen force. Gasps escaped all three of our lips.

"Why'd you ask it to do that, Athena!?" Justin yelled, his voice laced with panic.

"Curiosity got the better of me!" I gasped in response, equally startled by the movement.

"Maybe it's time to call it a night with this ghost business," Beth suggested cautiously.

Justin and I both nodded in agreement. We were about to utter our goodbyes when a loud, insistent banging echoed from the front door, abruptly cutting us off.

A collective scream tore from our throats.

"Goodbye!" I blurted out hastily.

The planchette on the Ouija board slowly moved across the letters, spelling out "goodbye," but the banging at the door continued relentlessly.

"We said goodbye! Why won't it leave us alone?" Beth questioned, bewildered.

"Maybe we offended it somehow," Justin mused.

"How do you offend a ghost exactly?" I quipped sarcastically, my voice strained as the banging escalated in volume. "Should we Suggest its ethereal look is a bit too last season?"

Before anyone could respond, the door splintered inwards, bursting open with a bang. We all let out bloodcurdling screams as a figure clad in a black hoodie stepped through the doorway.

My reflexes kicked in and I lunged for the hidden bow and arrows I kept under the couch, aiming them at the intruder. He threw his hood back, revealing a familiar face.

"What the heck is going on here!?" he exclaimed.

Relief washed over me as I recognized him. I lowered my weapons and started playfully punching his arm. "You nearly scared me to death!"

"Ouch!" he yelped, rubbing his arm. "I caught the scent of rogues and thought you were in danger."

"Hold on," I stopped hitting him, "these are my friends, Justin and Beth. They're rogues, but the good kind."

Hayden's brow furrowed in confusion. "What? I thought you hunted rogues."

"I have," I admitted. "But I've met some good ones over the years, and I trust these two completely." I gestured towards them with a reassuring smile.

"Hi," Justin greeted him nervously.

Hayden's gaze narrowed as he scanned Justin. "Why's there another male here with you?" he growled possessively.

"He has a mate, and he's gay," I explained simply.

"Oh. Sorry about that," Hayden mumbled, offering an apology to Justin.

Justin simply waved his hand dismissively.

"So, Hayden, what brings you here?" I asked.

"I came to apologize," he confessed. "Is there somewhere private we can talk?"

I nodded and turned to the twins. "Hey guys, can you put that Ouija board back downstairs?"

Beth shoved the board towards Justin with a playful nudge. "You got it."

Without another word, she stormed off in the direction of her room.

I grabbed Hayden's hand and practically dragged him to my room. Slamming the door shut behind us, I grumbled, "You owe me a new door."

"I'm truly sorry," he began, his voice filled with remorse. "About everything. You're going into heat, that's why I wanted to mark you. The full moon is coming up, and my wolf wanted to take you by force. I'm so sorry for scaring you." He nuzzled his face affectionately into my neck.

Wait a minute... that's why I have a fever?

Heat?

Guess there's no way around it then. It was going to happen sooner or later, and thanks to my traitorous body, it seems like sooner is now.

I hugged him back. "I'm sorry for yelling at you. I should have let you explain first."

"It's my fault. I should have told you you were going into heat," he admitted.

I sighed. "Mark me."

He looked at me with concern. "Are you sure? I don't want to force you."

I nodded in response. "I'm sure."

He smiled and leaned in, softly kissing my lips. I kissed back. He pulled away, his lips moving from my jaw to the sensitive spot where my neck met my shoulder. It took all my willpower not to let out a moan.

He focused on that spot, and I let out a moan as I felt him smirk against my skin.

He sucked on that spot, and I could feel his teeth sink in slightly. The initial discomfort was quickly replaced by a moan as he licked and kissed the area.

All the energy drained from my body. He picked me up bridal style and gently placed me down on the bed.

"Goodnight, princess," he whispered, kissing my forehead before I drifted off to sleep.

CHAPTER TEN

~Athena~

I woke up and my neck was stiff. Midnight was licking my face.

I set her down on the floor as she ran out of the room.

There was an arm resting on my stomach. I turned around and saw the arm was connected to Hayden. A few strands of his brown hair were covering his eyes. I moved the strands of hair away from his face.

He slowly opened his eyes and smiled at me.

"Good morning Princess." He greeted.

"I am anything but a princess. "Ugh, seriously? How many times do I have to hear that?" I groaned.

"You're a princess to me." He winked.

"Oh please, that's so lame. Maybe I should start calling you 'Cheesy Ball' from now on." I rolled my eyes.

"Why?" He whined.

"Because it matches your personality."

He rolled his eyes. "You can call me Cheese Ball if I can call you Princess."

"Maybe." I got up from the bed and took a shower.

I noticed my mark was a black moon with a light red fire design in the middle.

After my shower, I brushed my teeth and got dressed in jeans and a blue top.

Hayden wasn't in the room anymore instead a note took his place.

Sorry Princess. I Got caught up in a meeting this morning, but I'll be back shortly. There's something I need to ask you when I get back. Oh, and by the way, I arranged for someone to come fix your door!
~Hayden

I went downstairs and the door was fixed. Like nothing happened.

I went to the living room and the Ouji board was still in the same spot as last night.

Justin.

That big baby.

I picked it up and bout it back in the basement. I clambered back upstairs to find Beth whipping up waffles. The moment I entered, she caught my scent, spun around, and flashed a knowing smirk.

 "What?" I blurted defensively.

Her finger darted towards a spot on her neck as she whispered a single word, "Mark."

I felt a flush creep up my cheeks. "Hush," I mumbled.

Her laughter echoed through the room.

"Where's Justin?" I finally managed to ask, trying to deflect attention. "Went to see his mate," she replied, a frown replacing her earlier amusement.

I walked over to her and hugged her. "I know your mate rejected you. I'm sorry he did. Just give me his name and I'll put an arrow through him."

She hugged me back and shook her head. "No. I don't want him dead. Even though he deserves it."

I felt something wet on my shoulder but I ignored it.

"I-I accepted his rejection." She choked out.

"Why? Who is he?" I asked as I pulled away.

"Alpha Mac."
"The alpha that abused you and Justin!?" I yelled.
She nodded. "We were only 16 when we left our pack. We shifted at 13 and everybody was afraid of us. Alpha Mac kept us weak with wolfsbane but we were still able to talk to our wolves. We are now both 19. Now when he found us in California he rejected me."
"I'm glad you told me. The moment I see him is the moment he dies."
She laughed. "I'm glad I have you as a friend."
"How bout we go do something? Get your mind off things." I suggested.
She nodded. "How did you know that my mate rejected me?"
"Justin told me." I blurted out.
"Remind me to kill him when we get back."
"Let's leave then." I took a waffle and turned off the stove.
I put food in Midnight's bowl and she ate it up.
I grabbed my keys and phone and headed out the door with Beth.
Talking to Hayden through our mind link, I sent, 'I'm going out with Beth. I'll be back soon and please don't send any guards."
I could do it now since he marked me.
'OK, be safe, and no promises about the guards.' He replied.
I'm pretty sure he was smirking.
Shifting my focus back to the road, I continued driving.
We soon arrived at a werewolf mall.

As we entered a guy walked up to us with blond hair and brown eyes.

"Luna. Alpha Hayden sent me." He said. "I'm Jax."

I groaned. "I told him no guards."

"Since when are mates known to listen?" Beth asked.

Jax growled and put me behind him. "Rogue. Stay behind me, Luna."

"She's my friend. I told Hayden she was coming with me." I explained.

"Oh sorry." He apologized.

"My name is Beth." She stretched her hand out and Jax took it.

He mumbled an apology to me, 'Sorry about that, Luna.'"

"Call me Athena. I don't know why Hayden send me a guard, he knows I can protect myself." I complained.

"Whatever. Let's just shop." Beth smiled and started dragging me.

After hitting a couple of stores we decided to hit the food court.

"How about pizza?" I asked.

"Sounds good." Beth agreed as Jax nodded.

We arrived at the pizza place. The waiter greeted us and took our order. We opted for a giant pepperoni, enough to feed an army.

"Excuse me, I'll go pay," I announced, leaving the table.

I settled the bill at the register and headed back, accidentally bumping into someone on the way.

"My apologies," I mumbled.

Looking up, I met a smug face. Wait, what?! How is he here? He can't be alive! I took care of that.

"Damon?" My voice barely escaped my lips.

"Athena! Alpha's calling us!" Jax bellowed from the entrance.

I glanced back at Damon, but he vanished into thin air. Confused, I rejoined Beth and Jax.

Beth furrowed her brow and asked, "Is something wrong? You look spooked."

I offered a weak nod. "Yeah, I'm fine. Let's just get out of here."

We returned to my place, my mind a whirlwind of thoughts. Pushing them aside, I focused on the present when we arrived. Jax had already departed.

Entering the dimly lit house, I noticed a trail of flower petals leading towards the living room.

"Guess that's my cue to leave," Beth said, heading for her room.

Curiosity piqued, and I followed the trail. At the end stood Hayden, looking dapper in a tuxedo. Damn, he cleaned up well.

Hold on! No! I shouldn't be thinking that way!

Midnight, sporting a cute blue dress, stood beside him. How did he manage that?

"If this is a proposal, the answer's a hard no," I declared, approaching him.

He chuckled, but his expression quickly shifted to nervousness. Interesting.

"I was wondering if you'd like to go out on a date?" he stammered.

His awkwardness made me smile.

Wrapping my arms around his neck, I replied, "I'd love to."

He grabbed my waist, spinning me around. "Good. It would've been super awkward if you said no."

Setting me down, he planted a quick kiss on my lips.

"Alright, spill it. How did you and those twins meet?" I questioned.

"Long story. Up for it?"

"Hit me. I can handle anything." He puffed out his chest, flexing his muscles.

"All I see is muscle mass. Weakling much?" I teased, poking his arm.

Suddenly, he hoisted me into a bridal carry. My arms instinctively wrapped around his neck.

"This weak?" he smirked.

"Maybe just a tad," I conceded.

A smile crept across his face, and he captured my lips in a kiss. Sparks flew. I kissed back but denied him entrance when he grazed my bottom lip with his tongue. He groaned playfully.

Just then, a familiar voice interrupted our moment.

"Hey Athena, I was wondering if—" Justin began, then trailed off. "Oh, am I interrupting something?"

Hayden set me down. I glared at his smug grin. Jerk.

"No, Justin! What's up?" I inquired.

"Uh, right! I was wondering if, maybe, my mate and I could join your pack?" He felt nervous.

"Hayden, what do you think? I trust them," I declared.

Hesitation flickered across his face. "I don't know."

Taking his hand, I dragged him towards the kitchen.
"Agree with me, and unlock a month's worth of kisses."
He pouted. "Fine, they can join."
A triumphant smile spread across my face.
"On one condition," he smirked. "Unlimited kisses for a month."
"Why does there always have to be a catch?" I muttered under my breath. "Alright, fine."
Can't believe I just agreed to that.
Beaming like an idiot, he planted a kiss on my cheek.
Returning to the living room, I announced, "You've been accepted into the pack."
Justin grinned and pulled me into a hug. Hayden grumbled, but I ignored him.
Pulling away from Justin, I noticed a mark on his neck. Turning his head, I lifted a section of his shirt.
"Is that a bite mark, by any chance?" I smirked.
He swatted my hands away. Pretty sure he's blushing.
"Maybe," he mumbled, cheeks flushed.
My laughter erupted.
"Don't laugh! You have a mark yourself," he countered, a playful glint in his eyes.
That shut me up.
"Oh, whatever."
He laughed and then went up to his room.
I felt arms go around me. I turned around and saw Hayden grinning.
"Just out of curiosity, how did you get that dress on Midnight?" I asked.

He groaned. "That dog doesn't like me."
I laughed at him as Midnight started barking.
There was still one question running through my mind.
How is Damon here!?

CHAPTER ELEVEN

~Athena~

"So, brainstorming time," Hayden suggested, "how about a ceremony in two weeks to welcome Beth, Justin, Johnny, and you?"

"Wait, me too!?" I burst out, surprised.

We were at my place, sprawled on the couch. Our date was tomorrow, but Hayden wanted to spend some quality time today. Beth and Justin were at Johnny's, getting acquainted.

"Indeed. Since you've been marked, it's time for the pack to officially acknowledge you as their Luna."

"Wait, what? They don't know what I do!"

"Um, I don't think introducing me to your pack is the best idea," I stammered.

His expression fell. "Why not?"

"Because I'm a hunter," I stated as if it were obvious.

"Right, I forgot." He looked down, contemplating.

"Look, I trust my pack," he said, his gaze meeting mine. "I think we should be upfront with them. No one outside the pack will be the wiser. And if they don't accept you, well, they'll have to answer to me." A hopeful glint flickered in his eyes.

Should I go along with this? No outsiders would know. But was I ready to reveal my secret?

I hesitated. "Alright, fine," I conceded. "But complete secrecy outside the pack. No exceptions."

"Consider it done. Their discretion is assured," he offered a reassuring smile. "Speaking of, how about I introduce you to the beta, third in command, and their mates at the pack house?"

I shrugged. "Sure, why not? I'm free."

He chuckled as we made our way to the pack house.

••••

We entered the pack house. Everything seemed unchanged, except for the window I'd broken through - now fixed.

Stepping into the living room, we found Xavier and Robert lounging on the couch with their mates. The air crackled as they caught my scent, their eyes widening in shock.

"Athena?" Robert stammered.

"Please don't kill me," Xavier whimpered.

"No promises," I replied playfully.

He looked like he might faint.

"Just kidding," I added, maybe not entirely seriously.

"Guys, meet my mate, Athena. She's aware of our little secret," Hayden introduced me.

"Hi, I'm Jamie," a girl with dirty blonde hair and brown eyes greeted me with a wave.

"Summer here," another girl with blue hair and blue eyes chimed in, waving as well.

"Hold on, how do you know about us?" Robert demanded.

We settled onto the couch across from them.

"Remember Robin Hood?" Hayden started.

Xavier yelped, "The woman who shot me in the ass with an arrow? Yeah, I remember!""Oops, my bad. But in my defense, you were trying to ambush me," I countered.

It took a moment for them to click. Their eyes widened comically. Summer burst out laughing.

"Xavier complained like a baby after that arrow came out! Poor guy couldn't even use a chair for a while," she chuckled.

Laughter filled the room as Xavier pouted, glaring at us all.

When things calmed down, I spoke up. "Introductions aren't necessary. I have a file on each of you."

"What!?" Robert exclaimed.

"Part of my job involves receiving information files on the pack members whenever I'm assigned to a new location. Look, I pretty much have you guys figured out. It might sound creepy, but it comes with the job, you know?"

"Prove it," Summer challenged. "Who's my mate? Robert or Xavier?"

"Xavier," I answered confidently. "And Robert, you're with Jamie."

"What's my favorite color?" Jamie asked.

"Orange," I replied.

"What color is my wolf?" Robert inquired.

"Tan coat speckled with brown and eyes the color of the sea," I stated.

"Third in command or beta?" Xavier questioned.

"Third in command."

"She answered them all correctly," Hayden observed.

"Scared or not?" Xavier mumbled.

"Scared you should be. Another arrow in your ass is a breeze for me," I teased.

He jumped back, clutching his backside.

"Wimp," I muttered under my breath.

"Now that you're marked, is there a specific ceremony planned for your introduction to the pack?" Summer questioned.

"Two weeks," Hayden answered on my behalf. "We're bringing in three others first, then formally introducing Athena."

They both nodded. Checking his phone, Hayden said, "I gotta set up for our date tomorrow. You good getting home on your own?"

I gave a small nod as he planted a quick kiss on my lips before leaving.

Summer and Jamie exchanged playful smirks. "Date night, huh?" Jamie asked a hint of excitement in her voice.

Another nod from me was met with excited squeals from both of them. Robert and Xavier, bless their hearts, attempted to shield their ears from the noise.

"Last shopping trip?" Jamie pressed.

"Just a few days ago," I replied.

"Perfect! Let's head over to your place and pick out an outfit," she declared, grabbing my arm with a playful tug. Jamie and Summer practically dragged me out of the pack house, with me offering directions along the way.

Back at my place, I found Justin and Beth had returned. Introductions were made, and now Beth was joining the hunt for the perfect outfit with the other two. Fantastic.

••••

Clad in a blue dress layered over black leggings and a leather jacket (I stubbornly insisted on my blue Converse), I stood before the mirror, barely recognizing myself. Summer had picked out the outfit, Jamie had styled my hair, and Beth had applied mascara, lip gloss, and a touch of eyeliner.
"Jordan is going to be howling at the moon with desire the moment he sees you," Summer remarked with a mischievous grin.
"Who's Jordan?" Beth asked, confused.
"His wolf," I explained.
Glancing at Midnight for her opinion, I saw her tail wagging excitedly. Yep, she approved. As if on cue, Jamie's eyes glazed over.
"Hayden's here," she announced with a knowing grin.
A smile crept across my face as I headed outside. Hayden leaned casually against his car, looking sharp in a black dress shirt and blue jeans.
Ugh, why did I have to find him so attractive? Shaking off the thought, I greeted him with a playful, "Hey Cheese Ball."
His gaze met mine, his eyes briefly flashing black before settling on their usual mismatched colors.

"You look stunning, Princess," he breathed, sending a wave of warmth through me.

"Not too bad yourself," I countered.

He smiled warmly and opened the car door for me, a gesture I waved away.

"I can handle it," I pointed out.

"I know you can, but I just wanted to do something nice." He leaned in for a quick peck on my cheek as I climbed into the passenger seat.

Once settled, he started the engine. "I told my grandparents about the date, by the way. Grandma was thrilled, Grandpa wanted to shoot you with an arrow."

Breaking the silence that followed, I asked, "Where are we going?"

"Surprise," he smirked.

"Ugh, I don't like surprises," I groaned playfully.

"Because they're fun," he said, his smirk unwavering.

The car came to a stop in front of the familiar forest clearing – the place where we'd first met. A table draped in a white cloth stood in the center, adorned with three candles and two chairs facing each other.

"The scene of the crime, huh?" I smirked, referring to our initial encounter.

"Crime?" he chuckled. "Meeting you was the best day ever in my entire life."

"Yeah, well, it was also the day you stole my gold coin and snuck into the back of my truck."

He winked at me before leaning in for a kiss on the cheek. "But I kept coming back, didn't I?"

"You are my Cheese Ball," I conceded playfully.

He gestured for me to take a seat, which I did. A waiter appeared and took our orders. I opted for a classic greasy burger and fries, while Hayden, to my amusement, chose a steak with a side salad. Can you believe him?

The waiter winked at me before he left, prompting a playful kick from Hayden under the table (or so I'm pretty sure that's what happened). The waiter groaned and scurried off, earning him a glare from me.

"What?" Hayden feigned innocence.

"Don't play dumb. You hurt him," I accused.

"He winked at you!" he growled possessively. "You're mine."

A playful eye roll escaped me. "Drama king," I teased.

The waiter returned with our food. Hayden shot the server a withering glare.

I mirrored Hayden's glare, but he just flashed a wide, toothy grin.

With another roll of my eyes, I dug into my meal.

After finishing our food, Hayden took my hand and led me deeper into the woods.

"There's no cause for alarm," he chuckled. "Let's just say, if I had any bad intentions, the day we met would have been the perfect chance to act on them.

I smirked. "And how'd that little plan go for you?"

He countered with a roll of his own eyes before continuing.

We soon arrived at the clearing where he'd planned his ambush.

"What brings us back here?" I inquired.

He gestured towards the tree where I'd shot Xavier. "Look," he said with a smile.

I followed his gaze to the tree trunk, where a heart with "H+A" carved inside was proudly displayed.

"Maybe I am a bit cheesy," he admitted as he wrapped his arms around me from behind.

My energy seemed to seep away, and I felt Hayden lift me into his arms bridal style. Leaning my head against his chest, sleep peacefully claimed me.

CHAPTER TWELVE

~Athena~

I'd filled my grandparents in on the ceremony. Initially, they weren't thrilled about the entire pack knowing about me, but the future Luna title did tend to change their perspective. It still felt strange calling myself that – Luna.

The plan was for me to make my entrance as Robin Hood after Beth, Justin, and Johnny's official induction. Nervous butterflies swarmed my stomach. What would it be like?

Beth, Summer, and Jamie were all decked out in dresses. Beth sported a beautiful blue and white number – a white top flowing into a blue skirt. Her hair was straightened, and white wedge sandals completed the look. Summer opted for a sleek black off-the-shoulder long-sleeved dress that hit mid-thigh, accented by two sheer panels at the waist. Her hair was styled in a curly bun, and black heels added a touch of elegance. Jamie went with a dark blue two-piece dress with a sweetheart neckline and a knee-length skirt. Her hair flowed freely, and black wedges grounded her outfit.

Midnight, meanwhile, was at the pack house with Hayden, sporting a rather unusual accessory – a red plaid dress with a black bow! I knew it might seem silly to dress up a dog, but Midnight honestly didn't seem to mind.

We'd all gotten ready at my place. The thought of how the pack members would react to seeing me twisted in my gut.

"Alright, time to head to the pack house!" Jamie's voice snapped me out of my thoughts.

"You guys go ahead," I mumbled, a bit hesitant. "I'll walk."

They gave a quick nod and disappeared down the street. Taking a deep breath, I set off for the pack house, the weight of the ceremony pressing down on me.

~Hayden~

Everything was prepped and ready. I couldn't wait to introduce my mate to the pack. Beth, Justin, Johnny, along with the usual crew of Xavier, Robert, Summer, and Jamie, were all present. Midnight, feeling a bit out of place, found a comfortable spot with one of the guards by my side. We were just waiting for the pack members to arrive.

People started filing in, filling the designated seats. The ceremony couldn't begin until Athena arrived, and concern gnawed at me as I couldn't see her anywhere.

"Any idea where Athena is?" I asked Beth, hoping for a reassuring answer.

"Nope, she wasn't with us," Beth replied.

Reaching out through the mind link, I sent a message to Athena, "Princess, where are you?"

Her reply came quickly, "On my way. Just start without me."

"Are you sure?" I questioned, unsure if it was the best course of action.

"Positive. Start as soon as everyone's here."

Before I could respond further, the mind link went silent. The last stragglers entered with their pups, finding their seats, and with a deep breath, I initiated the ceremony.

"Welcome, Midnight Fire Pack! Today, we have the honor of inducting three new members – Beth Wood, Justin Wood, and Johnny Carson. Please extend your right hand."

With a gesture, they all followed my instructions. Taking a small blade, I made a clean cut across my palm and mirrored the action on theirs. As we joined hands, the wounds instantly began to heal, and I felt them connect through the pack bond forming in our minds.

"Congratulations! You are now all officially part of the Midnight Fire Pack," I declared to a room filled with applause.

While the applause subsided, I took a moment to reconnect with Athena through the mind link. "Athena, are you here yet?"

"Just keep going," she responded, followed by a mental block shutting me out.

Waiting for the sound of clapping to die down, I continued. "There's one more thing. I've found my mate, and she will be your Luna. I expect you to treat her with the utmost respect, just as you treat me. Please join me in welcoming your Luna!"

Suddenly, a figure crashed through the window, landing gracefully on one knee on the stage. It was Athena, dressed in full Robin Hood attire! She rose to her feet, ignoring the growls and snarls erupting from the pack members and guards.

"Silence!" Grabbing the microphone, I raised my voice to a commanding level, bringing immediate silence as the crowd instinctively covered their ears.

Lowering my voice, I addressed the pack, "This is my mate."

The room remained quiet until Athena confidently began to speak.

"For many of you, I'm the notorious Robin Hood, a hunter. You've heard rumors and stories about me, whispers of how I kill any werewolf I encounter. Let me assure you, those rumors are false. My targets are rogue werewolves, a fact that doesn't erase the fact that I am a killer. Earning your trust will be a journey, but I'm taking a leap of faith by revealing my secret to you. Nobody beyond this pack knows my true identity. Please, keep it that way."

With a dramatic flourish, she removed her hood and mask, revealing her face to the pack for the first time.

"My name is Athena King," she declared, her voice ringing clear. "And I vow to protect this pack with my very life."

A wave of pride washed over me as she demonstrated the courage to finally reveal herself. 'She's right, you are cheesy,' Jordan teased through the mind link.

'Shut up. You ruined the moment,' I grumbled back playfully.

'Just doing my job,' his voice echoed in my head.

Despite the initial shock, the pack erupted in applause, whistles, and cheers. They were accepting her.

"We'll keep your secret, Luna!" someone from the crowd yelled.

A genuine smile spread across Athena's face as she acknowledged their response. 'You know, you just broke a window,' I said through the mind link, a hint of amusement in my voice. 'I think you owe me a new one.'

'Do I look like a window fixer?' she retorted playfully.

'Alright, alright, fine. Don't fix it.' With a chuckle, I took her hand and led her off the stage.

The moment we were out of sight, I couldn't resist pulling her in for a kiss.

She was surprised at first but quickly responded.

To my disappointment, she pulled away.

"What was that for?" She asked while smiling.

"Because I'm proud of you. You took off your mask." I smiled back.

"Hey, Hayden." My familiar voice popped in.

I turned around and saw Tiffiny. She's one of my closest friends.

"Hi Tiffiny." I greeted and turned back to my mate.

"Aren't you going to introduce me to your mate?" Tiffiny asked, a hint of amusement in her voice.

Turning towards her, I gestured to Athena. "Athena, this is one of my closest friends, Tiffiny. Tiffiny, this is my mate, Athena," I introduced them formally.

Athena offered a simple, "Hi," in greeting. Tiffiny responded with a friendly wave.

"I'll be right back," I announced, leaning down to plant a quick kiss on Athena's nose before heading off to find Midnight.

~Athena~

An awkward silence hung in the air. To ease the tension, I turned to Tiffiny and asked, "So, how long have you known Hayden?"

Her demeanor shifted instantly. "Let's get this straight," she declared, a sharp edge to her voice. "Hayden is mine."

My expression hardened. Of course, there had to be a hidden rival lurking beneath the friendly facade. "You must have bumped your head a few too many times as a wolf," I retorted, "because he's my mate."

Fury burned in her eyes. "He's mine! We were destined to be mates until you showed up. A hunter and a werewolf? Unthinkable!"

"Fantasy seems to be blurring the lines of reality for you, sweetheart," I countered.

"Listen closely," she hissed. "I'll get to the bottom of this. Why would he choose you over me? I'm supposed to be the Luna!"

"The only thing you're cracking is a distorted reflection," I shot back, perhaps a little too harshly. Even I had to admit, she was undeniably beautiful.

"You'll regret this, bitch," she spat before storming off.

Hayden returned, Midnight trotting happily beside him. "Can you keep an eye on her for a bit? I need some headspace," I requested.

"Everything alright?" he asked with concern.

I nodded curtly and headed outside. Donning my mask and hood, I ventured deeper into the woods, seeking solitude. The sound of leaves crunching underfoot, a flicker of movement just out of sight, snapped me to attention. Ignoring it, I kept walking. Finally, I reached for an arrow, knocking it on the string and aiming towards the sound.

"Show yourself, Damon!" I yelled, my voice echoing in the darkness.

A figure emerged from the shadows, a smirk playing on his lips. "Missed me, baby?"

~Beth~

The cheers for Athena had barely faded when a captivating scent filled my senses - strawberries and pine. It seemed to have a life of its own, drawing me deeper into the pack house. Following the trail, I arrived at a doorway. As I raised my hand to knock, the door swung open, revealing a handsome man with dark hair and brown eyes.

"Mate! Mate! Mate!" Lexi screamed in my head, her voice filled with excitement.

The man didn't hesitate, pulling me into a tight embrace. "Mine," A possessive growl erupted from him.

Another mate? This was impossible! Rejection was a harsh reality I'd already faced. The Moon Goddess rarely bestowed second chances.

"Who are you?" I managed to ask, my voice barely above a whisper.

"Tyler." His voice was husky as he trailed kisses down my neck, but I gently pushed him away.

"We need to talk, now!" I blurted out, my thoughts swirling in a frantic storm.

He gestured towards the bed. Locking the door behind him, I knew I had to tell him about Alpha Mac.

CHAPTER THIRTEEN

~Athena~

A smug grin stretched across his face as he uttered, "Missed me, baby?"

My blood turned to ice. "Don't you dare call me that, Damon! We were never anything close to that!" I bellowed, outrage coursing through me.

He remained unfazed, the smirk clinging to his lips like a second skin. "Just as fiery as I remember. Always admired that about you."

With narrowed eyes, I took him in. His once neatly styled brown hair was now a tangled mess. The familiar freckles remained, but his previously warm, grayish eyes now held a sinister glint. A jagged scar marred his neck, a chilling reminder of the past.

"How are you even alive?" My voice shook with disbelief. "I ended you!"

"Seems I had some assistance. Maybe your aim back then wasn't quite as impeccable as it is now," he taunted with a cruel edge.

"How did you find me?" I demanded, my mind racing to grasp the situation.

"Been searching for a while, Athena. Just a friendly reminder that you still belong to me. Still my girlfriend, still my mate."

"Lies!" I shrieked, the memory of his betrayal fresh and raw. "You never were either!"

A flicker of something akin to annoyance crossed his features before the smirk returned. "You belong to me, Athena, and I'll do whatever it takes to have you back."

Before I could react, he effortlessly dodged the arrow that flew from my bow. "Those tricks won't work on me anymore, sweetheart," he chuckled, the sound sending shivers down my spine.

Another arrow launched from my grasp, but with an almost unnatural agility, he caught it mid-air. With a mocking flourish, he blew a kiss on the arrow before vanishing back into the shadows.

Disgust roiled in my stomach. "Who was that?!" Hayden's voice, laced with a barely controlled rage, boomed from behind me. "Why'd he call you baby?"

I whirled around, catching a glimpse of the struggle between Hayden and his wolf for control. "Spying on me now, Hayden?" I snapped, irritation coloring my voice.

Ignoring my question, he pressed on, his voice a low growl. "Who was that guy?"

"Someone from the past," I mumbled, frustration building.

"Not if he called you baby and blew you a kiss," he countered, his possessiveness barely contained.

"Let's just say I'm thoroughly repulsed by him," I muttered, trying to deflect further conversation.

"You're mine, Athena. And I want him to know that. Now who was he?!"

The anger and frustration threatened to consume me. "That's enough. This is not up for discussion," I stated definitively, shutting down any further conversation.

With that, I stormed past him, my steps quickening as I headed back home. Collapsing onto my bed, I closed my eyes, the weight of the encounter pressing down on me. It had been a long, unsettling day.

Flashback

I laughed as Damon accidentally got his foot caught on a rope and is now hanging upside down by a tree.

All his arrows fell out of his quiver.

"Are you going to help me or what?" He asked while smiling.

I walked up to him. "I'm going to go with or what."

He groaned. "C'mon Athena-"

"Wait," I hushed him, my voice low. "Using our real names is a bad idea.."

"Why not?" He asked.

"Because If any rogues found out who we were, they'd be hunting us down instead."

"So what do we call each other?"

I light bulb went off in my head. "We need code names."

"What kind of code names?"

"Well we're both archers, so we need names of archers."

"Mine can be Apollo." He smirked.

"Apollo. That is so lame. You want to be named after Greek mythology?"

"I got one for you too." He avoided the question.

"Oh really? What is it then?" I asked.

"Robin Hood." He answered.

"Robin Hood? As in the guy who steals from the rich and gives to the poor?"

"Yep." He confirmed.

"Why Robin Hood?"

"Get me down now, and maybe I'll tell you why."

I smirked. I untied the rope from his leg and let him fall.

He groaned as he landed on his back.

"Now why would I want to be named after a guy archer in tights?" I asked.

"It'll be a Robin Hood unlike anyone's ever seen," he declared, standing tall after dusting himself off. I watched him with a skeptical expression, unsure of what to make of his words.

"You can make Robin Hood into a girl and show werewolves that she can be dangerous. That she can be more than some dude in tights. Show werewolves that she can be a killer."

I smirked.

Robin Hood.

It's starting to grow on me.

Flashback ends

That was my first day of hunting.

It was also the day Robin Hood was born.

Without Damon I'm pretty sure rogues would come after me as Athena.

But he betrayed me and lied to me.

We had a great thing going and he threw it away.

~Hayden~

Who was that guy!?

I saw it when he blew a kiss to her. It made my blood boil.

'At least she looked disgusted.' Jordan pointed out.

'That was the only thing that made me happy about the situation.'

'I heard her say his name was Damon. Maybe you can find out who he is.' Jordan hinted strongly.

"Good point, gotta hit the office first."

'Finally, you caught on.' Jordan muttered. 'Idiot.'

I rolled my eyes at him and made my way to my office.

'Robert, I need a favor.' I mind-linked him.

'Sure man. What do you need?'

'I need you to look up a rogue for me. His name is Damon. He has brown hair grayish eyes, freckles, and he has a scar across his neck.' I described him.

'OK, I'm on it.'

'Send the files to my office.'

I entered my office. Midnight was on my desk asleep.

I guess Summer put her in here. She didn't have her dress on anymore.

Despite being fast asleep, her eyes momentarily peeked open at my arrival.

I sat down on my chair. Midnight heard me and woke up.

"I don't suppose you know who Damon is do you?" I asked.

She growled at the sound of his name. I almost flinched.

'Wimp.' Jordan snickered.

I blocked him out.

"You know something about Damon don't you?" I asked

She growled again but nodded her canine head.

I was about to say something but Robert came in with a file in his hand.

"Take a look at this," he offered, placing the file in my hands.

"Thanks, Robert you can leave now."

He left as I started looking through the file.

Full Name: Damon Jake.

Age: 20

Rank: Rogue

Status: Deceased

'How is he dead if we saw him breathing?' Jordan asked.

'I don't know. But it looked like he had a history with Athena. She's keeping secrets from us.'

'Cut her some slack. There's plenty of stuff we haven't told her.' He defended.

"I understand, but for now, it's something I need to keep to myself."

'She might not be ready to talk about Damon yet either.'

'Why wouldn't she want to talk about it?'

'Didn't you see her? She seemed on the verge of tears. She never cries.'

'You're right.'

'I'm always right.' He smirked.

I blocked him out. Cocky much.

If Midnight growled at the mention of his name then she knows something about him.

I have to get talk to Athena.

I picked up Midnight and made my way out of my office. I was stopped by Tiffiny.

"Where are you going, Hayden? You just got back." She asked.

"Not now Tiffiny."

"Who's mutt is that?" She pointed to Midnight.

Midnight growled at her and bit her finger.

"Ow. Bitch." She muttered.

"This is Athena's dog. Midnight is not a mutt." I defended.

"That explains a lot. She taught her dog to be a bitch just like her." She whispered to herself.

It was my turn to growl. "Watch your mouth."

Her eyes turned red then gray then back to blue. She walked away without saying anything.

She never acted like this before. She's been moody ever since Athena got here. I've never seen her eyes red before.

'Maybe she's jealous.' Jordan thought.

'Why would she be jealous?' I asked.

He blocked me out. My steps quickened as I drew closer to Athena's place.

CHAPTER FOURTEEN
~Hayden~

Upon arrival at Athena's house, I found her unconscious on the bed, her bow lying discarded on the floor. Compelled to express my love, a feeling only previously confessed during her slumber, I gently placed Midnight down. As I reached to remove her quiver, Athena's hand darted from beneath her pillow, a silver knife flashing dangerously close to my face. The sight sparked a flurry of questions: since when had she adopted this under-pillow weapon strategy, and how had I missed it entirely? Reacting swiftly, I grasped her wrist, cautiously disarming her. The silver gleam of the blade was interrupted by my grip, and I placed the weapon on the side table. Her hand instinctively retreated under the pillow. Another attempt to retrieve the quiver was met with the same defensive maneuver, albeit this time without a weapon in hand. Frustration mounting, I secured the quiver and guided her hand back to the bed. Succumbing to the urge for closeness, I laid down beside her and pulled her into my embrace. She responded by nuzzling closer, a development that brought a smile to my face. A shift in her sleep was followed by the slow fluttering of her eyelids as she gazed up at me.

"Awake already, Princess?" I inquired, a grin lingering on my lips.

"Still tired," she mumbled, burrowing her head back into my chest.

"Speaking of which," I began, curiosity piqued, "how long has this under-pillow knife routine been in effect?"

"Sorry," she mumbled apologetically, "it's just a reflex. I didn't hurt you, did I?"

A smirk played on my lips. "Worried about me, are we?"

She offered a weak, "Maybe." in response.

A chuckle escaped my lips. "Relax, you didn't hurt me."

Relief washed over her as she whispered, "Good."

The seriousness returned to my voice as I asked, "Now, are you going to tell me about Damon, Athena?"

A flinch betrayed her at the mention of the name. "I don't want to talk about it."

"You know you can tell me anything," I reassured her. "I'm always here for you."

A tremor ran through her voice as she whispered, "Are you going to hurt me?"

Solemnly, I replied, "Never, Princess. Hurting you in any way is the furthest thing from my mind."

"Promise?" she pressed.

"I promise." My vow hung heavy in the air as I brushed a soft kiss on her forehead. "I do-"

The sound of my phone ringing abruptly cut me off. Annoyance bubbling within me, I answered the call with a sharp, "What!?"

"Hayden, I need your help!" Tiffany's voice shrieked through the receiver. "Rogues have surrounded me! They said they won't let me go unless you come get me!"

"Alright, calm down. Where are you?" I demanded.

"Near the south border," she replied frantically. "Please hurry!"

The call ended abruptly. Turning back to Athena, I apologized, "I'm so sorry, Princess, but something has come up. This won't take long. I'll see you soon."

With a simple, "Okay," she acknowledged my words.

A gentle kiss landed on her lips before I rose from the bed and exited the house. The faint scent of Tiffany filled the air, a detail that struck me as odd. Perhaps my nose was injured. As I prepared to take another step, a searing pain erupted in my neck. Instinctually, I reached up and grasped the source of the pain, pulling out a dart. A sniff confirmed my suspicions - wolfsbane. A low growl rumbled from within me, the voice of Jordan. Disorientation washed over me, my vision blurring at the edges. Black spots danced before my eyes, and the world began to fade. My body gave way, collapsing onto the ground. My eyelids grew heavy, and sweat beaded on my forehead. The last image that registered before succumbing to darkness was Tiffany smirking down at me, a beaker filled with a green liquid clutched in her hand. Then, oblivion.

~Athena~

Twenty-four hours had passed since Hayden last walked through my door. His promise of a swift return echoed hollowly in my mind. Where could he be? Was I becoming unreasonably attached?

A sudden burst of ringing shattered my introspection. Without bothering to check the caller ID, I answered with a simple, "Hello?"

"Athena, it's Robert. Have you seen Hayden?" His voice crackled with worry.

"No," I replied, the weight of his absence settling heavier. "He left yesterday and hasn't returned."

"We can't find him either. It's completely out of character for him to vanish without a word."

"When was the last you saw him?" I pressed.

"I dropped by the pack house with a file on a rogue named Damon Jake." A flicker of unease crossed his voice at the name. "Did he speak with anyone before leaving?"

"Hmm, let me think. He did have a brief conversation with Tiffany. She kept muttering something about rabies and Midnight." A frown creased my forehead. "Then I saw him leave with her."

"And Tiffany? Have you seen her since?"

"Not a trace. She disappeared shortly after Hayden."

"This is getting suspicious," Robert declared. "We should probably wait a bit longer, but if they don't show up soon, we'll need to organize a search party."

"Right," I agreed. "But why meet at the pack house? Shouldn't-"

"You're the Luna, Athena. In the Alpha's absence, his duties fall to you."

"Oh," I mumbled, a pang of responsibility settling in my gut. "I'm on my way."

The call ended, leaving me alone with the silence. Midnight, oblivious to the brewing turmoil, gnawed contentedly on a chew toy.

"Did Hayden talk to Tiffany?" I asked her tentatively.

A low growl rumbled in her throat at the mention of the name, mirroring the reaction she usually reserved for Damon. Something was amiss.

"What is it, girl?" I pleaded. "Give me a hint."

Midnight trotted out of the room, returning moments later with a stuffed wolf toy clutched in her jaws. She dropped it at my feet and let out a sharp bark.

Wolf? "Midnight, I know Tiffany's a werewolf. She wouldn't be part of the pack otherwise. Vampires aren't exactly welcome."

She shook her head with a dismissive flick as if rejecting the notion.

"Alright, so not a werewolf," I pondered. "Then what exactly is she? And how come she still has a wolf companion?"

Once again, she disappeared downstairs, the rhythmic thud of her paws echoing on the wooden steps. A flurry of activity followed, the sound of rummaging filling the air. Curiosity piqued, I descended into the cool, dimly lit basement.

There I found Midnight, nose buried deep in a collection of boxes overflowing with relics from my childhood. She emerged triumphantly, a dusty chemistry set clamped in her teeth. Deftly navigating the stairs, she placed the kit before the stuffed animal with a satisfied bark.

A chuckle escaped my lips as I recognized the set. "This old thing? I used to think science was a form of magic."

A sharp bark, seemingly in agreement, erupted from Midnight.

"What? What did I just say?"

The barks continued, insistent and rapid.

"Magic?" I ventured, a spark of understanding flickering in my mind.

Another bark, a single, affirmative response.

"What does that mean?" Frustration tinged my voice.

A low growl, almost playful, rumbled from her throat before she retreated downstairs. Following her lead, I found her diligently pawing through the boxes once more. This time, she emerged with two articles of clothing firmly in her grasp.

"Midnight, what are those?" My question hung unanswered in the air. Her gaze remained fixed on the stairs, oblivious to my words. Climbing back up, she deposited the clothes at my feet before disappearing once more into the labyrinth of the basement.

Following her back upstairs, I watched as she meticulously arranged the clothing items in front of the chemistry set and stuffed animal. Recognition dawned on me - it was my old witch costume from Halloween, the one I wore when I was ten.

"Wolf. Witch. Magic?" I pointed at the items in sequence, my voice laced with confusion.

A long moment of silence stretched before a thought struck me. "A witch and werewolf hybrid?" The words tumbled from my lips in a hesitant murmur, more a question hanging in the air than a declaration.

A single bark from Midnight confirmed my suspicion.

"A magic spell cast by her?" I pressed, hope flickering in my chest.

Another affirmative bark. Tiffiny had put a spell on Hayden!

Fueled by urgency, I donned my hunter's attire and sprinted towards the pack house, Midnight keeping pace beside me. As I ran, I mind-linked the warriors: 'This is your Luna. I need some warriors stationed at the front of the pack house, but not the entire force. I'm on my way and will explain everything when I get there.'

Shifting gears, I mind-linked Robert specifically: 'Robert, did Tiffiny's eyes ever change into an unusual color?'

'Yeah,' his voice crackled in my head. 'If she was mad, her eyes would flash red.'

'Well, she's not a rogue,' I clarified. 'She's a witch and werewolf hybrid.'

'What?! How do you know?' came his astonished reply.

'Just meet me at the pack house with the warriors and Xavier. No time to explain!'

The packed house loomed into view, guards standing in a rigid line. Robert and Xavier barked orders, their voices carrying on the crisp air. As my scent reached them, heads snapped in my direction.

"Athena, what do you mean Tiffiny's a witch hybrid?" Robert demanded as I approached the group.

"Here, Xavier, can you take Midnight inside?" I pleaded, handing her over to the waiting Beta.

"Look, I know it sounds crazy, but-" I began, only to be cut off by a familiar voice.

The pack house door creaked open, revealing Tiffiny. A chilling smile played on her lips as she addressed me, "Well, well, well, if it isn't the little huntress herself." Beside her, Hayden stood like a statue, devoid of emotion.

"The jig is up, Tiffiny," I yelled, my voice ringing with newfound confidence. "I know you're a witch hybrid. Just confess!"

A devious smirk played on her lips. "Looks like you figured it out, huntress. No more playing pretend. I am, indeed, a witch hybrid."

A collective gasp rippled through the gathered warriors behind me.

"What do you want, Tiffiny?" I demanded, my voice hardening with anger.

"Just a little test," she replied, her tone dripping with amusement. "I want to see if Hayden would truly protect his precious huntress...from anything. Even himself."

Confusion clouded my features. "What the hell is that supposed to mean?"

"A simple spell," she explained, her eyes gleaming with malice. "Hayden has forgotten that you're his mate. Now, he'll attack anyone I tell him to, including you. You're both going to fight. No rules."

Fury bubbled within me. "What do you gain from this!?"

"A little entertainment," she purred. "This is a fight to the death, Athena. If Hayden defeats you, your life is forfeit, and I'll be Luna in your place. If you win, which is highly unlikely, you kill Hayden, breaking the spell. But either way, I get to see you shattered by the loss of your mate."

"And if I refuse?" I challenged, my voice trembling with a mix of fear and defiance.

"Then," Tiffiny purred, a cruel smile blossoming on her face, "Hayden gets rid of you. Right here, right now."

Silence stretched between us, thick with tension. Then, with a chilling command, Tiffiny pointed at me and ordered, "Hayden, that's a huntress. Kill her."

Hayden's eyes remained vacant, but his body obeyed. He charged towards me, a weaponless but deadly force.

CHAPTER FIFTEEN

~Athena~

A blur of motion – Hayden was charging towards me. With a desperate lunge, I dove to the side, narrowly avoiding the full force of his collision. The warriors around us surged forward, only to be halted in their tracks as Tiffiny flung a vial at their feet. A potent potion shattered on the ground, and her voice rang out, laced with menace, "She does this on her own, or you all die."

Eyes narrowed, I barked a command, "Stay where you are!"

"Athena, we can't just stand by and watch-" Robert began, but I cut him off sharply.

"That's an order, soldier. Don't move."

A bewildered growl rumbled from Hayden's throat. "Why are you giving orders? Why are they obeying you?" Confusion tinged his voice, a chilling sign of the spell's hold.

He had forgotten who I was.

He lunged at me again, a primal snarl curling his lip. This time, I was ready. With a practiced roll, I evaded his attack and whipped out my staff, the silver tip catching the sunlight momentarily. A solid whack connected with his back, eliciting a pained groan as he stumbled and rolled onto the grass, clutching his injured area. Thankfully, only the inner core of the staff, imbued with wolfsbane, was crafted from silver.

"Hayden, please," I pleaded, my voice laced with anguish. "I don't want to hurt you."

Rising with a feral snarl twisting his face, he roared, "Liar!"

Shoving my staff away, I met his gaze head-on, defying any fear that threatened to surface. He launched himself at me once more, but with practiced agility, I anticipated his move. Just as he came within reach, I placed my hands firmly on his chest and stomach, leveraging his momentum to send him tumbling over my back.

"Stop, Hayden! You're not thinking straight!" I cried out, desperation edging into my voice.

He rose again, but this time, a chilling title rolled off his tongue. "It's Alpha Hayden."

His fists flew at me in a flurry of rage. I managed to block most with my forearms, the blows sending jolts of pain up my arms, but at least they weren't landing on my face.

"Not to your mate, it's not!" I countered, hoping to jar some semblance of reason loose.

He shoved at me, but I held my ground. "You are not my mate! I haven't found my mate!" Denial laced his voice, a desperate attempt to cling to something familiar.

With a cunning move, he swept his leg under mine, sending me crashing to the ground. He loomed over me, a menacing shadow. Reacting on instinct, I fumbled for my bow and arrow, nocking it in place before letting loose a shot that found its mark in his shoulder. He let out a guttural cry, the sound raw and primal.

Regret flooded through me as I realized, in the heat of the moment, that I hadn't replaced my usual wolfsbane arrows with standard ones. "Oops," I muttered under my breath as I saw the wound slowly begin to heal.

"Yeah, right," he spat, his voice dripping with sarcasm despite the evident pain throbbing in his shoulder. "'You didn't want to hurt me'? Easy for you to say."

"You left me no choice," I countered, my voice taut with tension.

He shook his head, a flicker of frustration crossing his features, then lunged again. This time, he connected, sending me sprawling to the ground with him landing on top. A primal struggle ensued. I reached for my dagger sheath, but he reacted faster, pinning both my wrists to the ground beside my head.

"Trying to reach for your little knife to kill me?" he sneered. "You hunters are no better than rogues."

That was it. The final straw. His words ignited a fire within me, a surge of anger hotter than volcanic lava. With a burst of adrenaline-fueled strength, I slammed my feet into his stomach, pushing him off me. We both scrambled to our feet, the fight far from over. He came at me again, fists flying. One connected with a sickening crack, sending a jolt of pain through my nose. A groan escaped my lips as I reached up to clutch my throbbing nose, momentarily blinded and vulnerable. He seized the opportunity, landing a brutal kick to my legs, followed by a vicious punch to my stomach.

Another blow connected with my bottom lip, drawing a bead of blood.

The throbbing pain in my nose was unbearable. Gritting my teeth, I forced it back into place, a sharp cry escaping my lips as the bones clicked. Relief washed over me momentarily, only to be replaced by a surge of fresh panic as I saw Hayden holding aloft a familiar knife, a cruel smirk twisting his features. My gaze darted down to my holster, gaping open – my carelessness leaving me vulnerable.

Wasting no time, I snatched my staff, the familiar weight grounding me. He lunged at me, the wolfsbane dagger flashing in the sunlight. With a practiced twirl, I deflected the blow, the staff connecting with the blade with a loud clang. But the victory was short-lived. A searing pain erupted in my side, stealing my breath. Doubling over, I realized he had managed to slice through my waist, blood already staining my clothes and dripping down my leg.

Fueled by a surge of adrenaline, I lashed out with a powerful kick, catching him squarely in the chest and sending him flying backward. Without hesitation, I pressed the button on my staff, the wolfsbane blade extending with a menacing snick-snick. Hayden lay sprawled on the ground, groaning in pain, as I pinned him there with my foot on his chest.

The blade hovered inches from his throat. "Go ahead," he growled, defiance flickering in his eyes. "Kill me and prove me right."

I held his gaze for a long moment, the weight of the situation pressing down on me. Then, with a deep breath, I deactivated the blade, the wolfsbane retracting back into the staff. Holstering my weapon, I stood there, watching the confusion cloud his features.

"Why aren't you killing me?" he rasped, his voice laced with disbelief.

A tremor ran through my voice as I spoke, barely audible. "Because Hayden... you're my mate."

The anger that had momentarily subsided flared back up, erasing any trace of sympathy from his face. With a surge of strength, he grabbed my foot and shoved it off his chest. Caught off guard, I stumbled backward and fell onto the ground.

Seizing the opportunity, he lunged at me again, his hand wrapping around my throat with a bruising grip. Instinct taking over, I clawed at his wrists, gasping for air as my vision began to blur. Just as I reached the edge of unconsciousness, I forced myself to relax my grip, letting go of his wrists.

With a shaky hand, I fumbled with the zipper of my jacket, pulling the collar down to reveal the crescent moon mark etched on my skin. Then, with a trembling hand, I tore off the mask that had been hiding my identity.

The moment his gaze landed on the mark, a flicker of recognition sparked in his eyes, followed by a wave of shock. A look of pure horror contorted his features, his gaze locked on me with horrifying disbelief.

"It's your mark, Hayden," I rasped, struggling to speak with his hand still constricting my throat. "I'm your mate."

He remained silent for a moment, the weight of the revelation settling in. Then, a single word tumbled from his lips, barely a whisper. "Athena?"

The hostility drained from his face, replaced by a dawning comprehension. He slowly released his grip on my throat and offered me a hand to pull me up.

Mustering a weak smile, despite the throbbing agony, I offered a playful jab, "What, no Princess?"

Without another word, he pulled me into a tight embrace, his hold almost desperate. I felt him bury his head in the crook of my neck, his body shaking with silent sobs.

"I'm so sorry," he choked out into my shoulder. "So sorry. I hurt you."

Ignoring the dampness soaking into my clothes, I wrapped my arms around him, offering whatever comfort I could. "It's okay," I murmured. "You were under a spell. It wasn't your fault."

"But I knew what I was doing," he argued, his voice thick with remorse. "I couldn't stop myself. I hurt you."

I stroked his hair gently. "It's okay, Hayden. I don't blame you."

He pulled back slightly, his eyes filled with shame. "I'm such a bad mate."

Cupping his face in my hand, I forced him to meet my gaze. "No, you're not," I said firmly. "You're a good mate, and we'll get through this together."

Leaning in, I brushed my lips softly against his, careful not to aggravate my split lip. I pulled away.

"WHAT!?" Tiffiny yelled. "How did you break my spell!?"

'Grab her while she's distracted.' I mind linked the warriors.

"You little— let me go!" She yelled as the warriors grabbed her.

"Make sure she doesn't have any other potions. Take her to the cells." Hayden commanded.

They dragged her away. Hayden slammed his lips on mine again.

He snaked his arms around my waist. He accidentally touched my sliced flesh. I winced.

Pulling back, he met my gaze with a worried frown.

"Let's get you to the pack doctor." He picked me up bridal style.

"Hayden, you can't carry me. You're injured too." I pointed to his shoulder.

"Don't worry it's healing." He kissed my forehead and started walking to the pack hospital.

"You know what I just realized." I said

"What?" Hayden asked

"It was Alpha VS. Huntress. And the Huntress won." I smirked.

CHAPTER SIXTEEN

~Athena~

The doctor fussed over my lip, cleaning away the crimson stain. "Luna," the doctor said with a final check, "your lip is still bleeding a bit, but it should stop shortly. You're good to go whenever you're ready."

"Thank you," I breathed gratefully as she disappeared out the door.

We were in the pack doctor's office, thankfully. Luckily, Beth had stopped by with a fresh change of clothes, and Midnight was safely back at the pack house with the pups.

The moment the doctor left, Hayden leaned in and pressed a soft kiss to my cheek. "I can't believe I almost…" He trailed off, unable to finish the horrifying thought, and rested his head heavily on my shoulder.

"For the last time, Hayden," I insisted, "it wasn't your fault."

"Doesn't matter," he countered, his voice thick with guilt. "I hurt you, my mate. And I did it without even telling you…" His voice trailed off, a question hanging heavy in the air.

Confused, I furrowed my brow. "Telling me what?"

He stepped back, his gaze locking onto mine. Then, in a swift movement, he closed the gap between us and pressed his lips to mine.

"Are you sure that's a good idea?" I managed a weak laugh, the throbbing in my lip a constant reminder of the fight.

"Doesn't matter," he murmured, his voice husky with emotion, before capturing my lips in another kiss. "I love you."

The words hung in the air, heavy and unexpected. Did he just say…? A whirlwind of emotions swirled within me. Did I love him? Maybe I did…

"You don't have to say it back," he mumbled against my lips, his voice laced with a hint of vulnerability. "I just wanted you to know."

And with that, he vanished out of the room, leaving me speechless and reeling from his sudden confession.

I scrambled to my feet and chased after him, but he was already gone. We walked in silence back to the pack house, the weight of his words hanging heavy between us. He disappeared into his room, slamming the door shut behind him.

Desperation gnawed at me. "Hayden, please open up!" I pleaded, knocking on the door with increasing urgency. But there was no answer.

Defeated, I slumped against the cool wood of the door, tears welling up in my eyes. "Hayden," I whispered, my voice thick with emotion, "I thought I loved someone. But then he kept a huge secret from me, a lie that shattered my heart. I never thought anyone could heal that wound. But you did, Hayden. As cheesy and corny as it sounds, you did. I love you."

Silence. Then, a faint click from the other side. The door creaked open, and I tumbled forward, having forgotten I was leaning against it.

"Who was he?" Hayden demanded, his voice surprisingly possessive as he helped me up.

I straightened my clothes, wiping away a stray tear. "Damon Jake," I answered, my voice steady despite the tremor in my heart.

The sound of a low growl rumbled from his chest. He pulled me closer, his grip firm yet gentle. "Mine!" he declared possessively.

A wave of nausea washed over me as I inhaled deeply. This was it, the moment of truth. "Come, sit down," I said, ushering him towards the bed. He obeyed, but instead of sitting next to me, he pulled me onto his lap, his arms wrapped protectively around me.

"He was my best friend," I began, the memories flooding back. "We were inseparable. I even confided in him about my parents' death, telling him they were killed by rogues when I was just a year old. This gold coin," I held up the cherished token, "belonged to my mother. It's incredibly special to me. And he told me the same thing happened to his parents. Naturally, my grandparents thought we'd make perfect hunters. And we agreed. He even came up with our hunter names – mine was Robin Hood, and his, Apollo. Cheesy, right?" A humorless laugh escaped my lips.

"Anyway," I continued, needing to get everything out, "one day he claimed he was sick and couldn't hunt with me. Worried, I went alone. That's when I saw him — a sandy blonde wolf transforming right before my eyes. It was Damon. All along, he'd lied about being human."

~Flashback~

I was hiding in a tree. Waiting for the Sandy blonde wolf to shift back into human form.

They went behind a tree and came back as… Damon!?

He's a werewolf!?

He always told me about how much he hated werewolves.

I jumped down from the tree and landed right in front of Damon.

He loomed at me with a shocked and scared expression while I had a death glare.

"Athena I-I thought-" I cut him off.

"You thought what Damon!? You thought I wouldn't find you in wolf form!?" I yelled.

"I can explain."

"There's nothing to explain! You lied to me! Are you in a pack!? Are just spying on me for more information on other hunters!?"

"No! I'm a rogue! My parents were killed by our alpha! Why do you think I kept trying to get you to go after the wolves in packs!? I want them dead! I want my old alpha dead!" He growled.

"That's no excuse, Damon! You told me you were human! You were just using me just so you can get revenge on your old alpha!?"

"It started that way." He seemed more calm now. "Over time, I came to develop deeper emotions for you. I thought that there was a chance you might be my mate. My wolf told me that you weren't but I didn't listen to him. I love you, Athena!"

"I thought I loved you too. But I was wrong I do t love you. It's just my lust. I'm sorry Damon but I can't be with you."

He growled and attempted to punch me but I caught his fist in mid-air.

"I'm sorry Damon."

He released his fist from my grip and kept throwing punches at me.

I blocked them with my forearms but it still hurt.

He attempted to kick my head but I ducked under his leg and kicked his back.

I grabbed an arrow and shot his leg. He groaned and backed away from me.

I took more arrows and shot his stomach, legs, and arms.

He kept backing away until his back hit a bolder blocking him from moving.

He pulled out all the arrows from his body.

"If they're so evil, what makes you any different, Damon?" I tried staying calm. "You killed your kind."

"What makes you so different? You killed my kind?" He smirked.

"I'm human."

I answered before he took an arrow and sliced his throat with it.

~Flashback over~

"That's what happened. I saw him die right in front of me. Yet somehow he's here and alive." By now my eyes were filled with tears.

~Hayden~

I was silent. Trying to take in all the information she told me.

She was crying into my chest. I pulled her closer.

I've never seen her cry before.

"I killed my best friend." She sobs.

"You had a good reason." I cooed in her ear wile stroking her hair.

She shook her head. " I can't justify what I did."

I kissed her lips. "It doesn't matter anymore it's all in the past."

She wiped her tears away, then put her face on my neck.

'I don't know about you, but I'm getting turned on.' Jordan smirked.

'Anything our mate does gets you turned on.'

'What can I say? She makes me want to punish her.' His smirk stayed in place.

I blocked him out and turned back to my mate.

She was falling asleep. "I love you, Hayden."

"I love you too."

I helped her onto the bed and tucked her in.

I laid down next to her and pulled her into my chest.

I slowly drifted off to sleep.

CHAPTER SEVENTEEN

~Hayden~

A jolt of awareness ripped me awake, the expanse of the bed disconcertingly empty beside me. Panic surged, a cold fist squeezing my gut. My eyes darted around the room, taking in every detail: the closed closet door, the silent bathroom, even the illogical dip under the bed. The absence hung heavy, a suffocating silence where her presence should have been. Following the faint trace of her scent, I made my way downstairs, the path leading straight to the kitchen. There she was, diligently assembling a sandwich. My approach startled her, her body tensing before relaxing in recognition.

'Hey,' she greeted, turning around with a smile.

'Why weren't you in bed? I was a little bummed,' I admitted.

'Life doesn't always cooperate,' she joked.

Taking a deep breath, I blurted, 'Um, would you consider moving in with me? No pressure, of course, if you think things are moving too fast, or if-' Cutting me off with a playful hand over my mouth, she chuckled. 'Slow down, Mr. Rambler. English, please.' Her smile widened. 'Honestly, living together wouldn't be a big change. We practically do already.'

Overcome with joy, I scooped her up in a celebratory spin. My grin must have been ridiculous, but I couldn't help it. Setting her down gently, I declared, 'Excellent! Now go grab your things.'

'And who, pray tell, will be sorting my underwear drawer?' she questioned with a raised eyebrow.

A smirk played on my lips. 'Me.'

'Oh, you wouldn't dare,' she warned playfully.

Leaning in, I planted a kiss on her nose. 'I'll see them eventually.'

'Later the better, pervert,' she countered with a playful shove.

A chuckle escaped my lips. 'Speaking of missing members, where's Midnight?'

'Summer took her after yesterday's "win the pups" competition,' I replied.

She nodded in understanding just as our lips met in a kiss. As we pulled away, a voice echoed in my mind - a guard's mind link.

'Alpha, we apprehended a rogue trespassing on our territory this morning. He's currently secured in the cells.'

My growl rumbled in my chest. 'And you wait until now to inform me?'

'W-we apologize, Alpha,' the voice stammered, 'but you were still asleep.'

'Just keep him contained until I get there,' I instructed, sighing in frustration.

Turning back to my mate, I announced, 'Duty calls. Rogue interrogation.'

'Can I come?' Her eyes sparkled with hope as she asked.

'Negative,' I replied firmly.

Her brow furrowed. 'Why not?'

'There are unmated males in the cells,' I explained with a hint of possessiveness.

'So? What's the difference?'

'I care,' I growled, the possessiveness turning territorial. 'No rogue is taking what's mine.'

'Ours,' Jordan corrected in my head.

Rolling my eyes inwardly, I refocused on my mate.

'You can keep saying that,' she countered, 'but I'll always maintain I belong to myself.'

A low growl rumbled in my chest. I pulled her close, my lips brushing the sensitive skin behind her ear.

'Mine,' I declared possessively.

'Alright, alright,' she conceded with a sigh. 'If it makes you that territorial, I'll stay put.'

A satisfied smile tugged at my lips. 'Good.' I leaned in and pecked her on the lips. 'Love you.'

'Love you too,' she murmured before I headed off towards the cells.'

~Athena~

Sinking onto a stool at the kitchen island, I devoured my sandwich in record time. Hours seemed to have stretched into an eternity since Hayden left. Boredom gnawed at me, the unfairness of it all simmering under my skin. Stuck here while he got to play with interrogations? Ugh!

Xavier sauntered into the kitchen, breaking the monotony. "Hey Athena," he greeted.

"Hey," I mumbled back. "Seen Midnight anywhere?"

"Off playing with the pups," he replied. "Whatcha doin' all by yourself?"

"Enjoying some riveting solitude," I said sarcastically. "Unless you count being stuck here while Hayden interrogates some rogue and has all the fun."

"You think that's fun?" Xavier raised an eyebrow.

"Hey, I've interrogated my fair share of rogues over the years," I countered.

"So it's like a hobby for you now?" he teased.

"Pretty much," I agreed with a playful nod.

Out of the blue, a solution came to me with the force of a lightning strike. "Are you thinking what I'm thinking?" I blurted out.

"That with all those chemicals scientists use, how do they keep their lab coats so pristine?" Xavier shot back with a smirk.

I stared at him, incredulous. "No, you goof! The commercial! Laundry detergent!"

Xavier feigned offense. Come on, don't blame me for wondering if it was just another clickbait."

Rolling my eyes, I elaborated on my plan. "The rogues wouldn't recognize me as Robin Hood, right? So, I could waltz in there and scare the answers out of them with my terrifying presence."

"Scary you are, I'll give you that," Xavier conceded. "What's the guarantee he'd crack and confess to you, though."

"Because," I declared with a smirk, "I'm the girl with a quiver full of silver arrows and a dagger to match. Wouldn't you talk?"

A flicker of amusement crossed Xavier's face. "Fair point."

Upstairs, I found my belongings, including my weapons thankfully retrieved with gloved hands, already moved in. Throwing on my hunter's gear, I headed purposefully toward the holding cells.

Of course, the guards wouldn't budge. "Sorry, Luna, but Alpha's orders," one explained sheepishly.

"I'm here to assist with the rogue interrogation," I declared. "If Alpha doesn't like it, that's on him. Now, let me in."

After a hesitant exchange, they finally relented. The stench that greeted me was a repugnant cocktail of blood, decay, and something distinctly unpleasant. Ignoring it, I marched forward.

"Hey babe," a rogue from one of the cells greeted me with a leer.

"Back off, scum," I retorted, my voice laced with steel.

He chuckled but thankfully backed down.

The sound of Hayden's raised voice led me to another cell. Inside, a rogue was chained to the wall, silver burning his skin. Two guards flanked Hayden, who held a menacing whip. The rogue's face was a canvas of blood, his body marred by whip marks.

"I'll ask you again! Who sent you!?" Hayden roared.

"And I'll tell you again, I ain't talkin'," the rogue spat back defiantly.

"Fine!" Hayden bellowed, throwing the whip down.

My eyes widened in horror as I realized what he was about to do. The rogue tensed, bracing for the impact.

In a flash, I shoved myself between them, my arm raised to shield myself from the blow. The whip wrapped cruelly around my forearm, pain lancing through me. Yanking it from Hayden's slack grip, I barked orders. "You two, upstairs! Now!" I pointed at Hayden. "You. With me. Now!"

Hayden growled under his breath but stormed out of the cell. I slammed the door shut behind him, my anger a simmering inferno.

"What are you doing down here? I told you I didn't want you in here!" he growled.

"And I ignored you," I shot back, my voice icy.

A guttural groan rumbled from Hayden's chest, frustration thick in the air.

"Explain yourself," I demanded, my voice laced with steel as I held the confiscated whip aloft. "Why did you resort to torture, Hayden?"

"Killing rogues is no different," he muttered through gritted teeth.

"It most certainly is!" My voice rose a notch. "I don't torture, Hayden. Taking a life is one thing, but inflicting pain to break someone is a whole new level of low."

He let out a defeated growl before stomping out of the room. Honestly, he throws tantrums worse than a toddler sometimes.

With a deep breath, I steeled myself and re-entered the cell. The rogue sat there, his face an unreadable mask.

"Why'd you stop him?" He rasped. A spark of surprise momentarily ignited in his eyes.

"Surprised, are we?" I countered, taking a seat in front of him.

"Yeah, kind of. You're Robin Hood, the infamous rogue slayer." A sardonic smirk played on his lips.

"Slaying and torture are not the same," I stated plainly. "Now, spill it. Why are you here?"

He sighed, the sound heavy with despair. "I was meant to deliver a message to the Luna of this pack, but that power-hungry Alpha wouldn't let me see her. Her name is Athena King."

"The message?" I pressed, leaning forward in anticipation.

"Can't tell anyone but her," he said, his voice barely a whisper.

"Why not?"

"The one who sent me threatened my pups. Threatened to kill them if I breathed a word to anyone else." His voice cracked with emotion.

"And your mate?"

"He… he's gone. Killed because I disobeyed an order once." This time, a single tear rolled down his cheek.

My heart ached for him. I couldn't let his pups be harmed because of this. Slowly, with a deep breath, I lifted my mask, revealing my face to him.

"I am Athena King," I stated calmly. "What's the message?"

His jaw dropped in shock. He blinked a few times, then spoke in a shaky voice.

"Your freedom is the key to your pack's survival. Submit to Damon and they will be left unharmed. However, defiance will be met with a swift and decisive attack."

"What are your pups' names?" I asked softly.

He hesitated, confused by the question, then mumbled, "Harmony and David."

"Beautiful names," I offered with a genuine smile. A flicker of hope sparked in his eyes, replaced by a fleeting smile as he murmured, "My mate picked them."

I replaced my mask, my voice firm as I spoke. "My heart aches for your pups. I understand what's at stake, and I promise to do everything I can to keep them safe."

With that, I approached the cell door and unlocked the silver chains binding his wrists. He rubbed his sore wrists, his eyes filled with gratitude.

"Thank you," he rasped. "I won't forget your kindness. And I'll keep your secret."

"I'll see what I can do to get you released and reunited with your pups," I replied before exiting the cell.

Finding Hayden sprawled on the bed, face buried in the pillow, I quickly changed and crawled in beside him. Running my fingers through his hair, I spoke softly.

"I got him to talk. Seems Damon threatened his pups, that's why he wouldn't speak to anyone but me."

A moment of silence stretched before he reached out, pulling me close. The warmth of his embrace spoke volumes as he muttered, "I'm sorry."

CHAPTER EIGHTEEN

~Athena~

"Sorry for what?" I questioned, trying to keep my voice calm.

"For upsetting you. I shouldn't have whipped him" He mumbled, avoiding eye contact.

"And who exactly deserves the apology, Hayden? Me, or the rogue you tortured?" I countered, raising an eyebrow.

He whined a petulant sound that wouldn't fly with a toddler, let alone a grown man. "Fine, fine, I'll apologize to him later."

I blinked eyebrow still firmly in place. "Later? You mean now?"

He groaned dramatically, letting his head fall onto my lap. "Ugh, do you have to be so difficult? Saying 'sorry' is like pulling teeth."

"Just go," I said, pushing him off my lap gently. "I need to change."

"Can I watch?" he smirked, a playful glint in his eyes.

"No," I replied bluntly. "Get out."

He chuckled as he left the room, but not before throwing a mischievous glance over his shoulder. Just in case, I locked the door behind him, knowing his penchant for trouble.

Swapping into a black top, gray jeans, white suspenders, and my trusty Converse, I headed downstairs. The kitchen, unfortunately, was where I made my first mistake. There, sprawled across the counter in a heated make-out session, was Beth. Midnight, clearly traumatized by the sight, I sat on the floor with her paws covering her eyes and ears.

"Oh dear God, my innocent eyes! Seriously, guys, this is the kitchen!" I shrieked in mock outrage, my arm flying up to cover my eyes. Peeking through my fingers, I saw Beth scrambling to her feet, she and the mystery man blushing furiously.

"Midnight, you can look now," Beth mumbled, clearly flustered.

The poor dog gingerly removed her paws, blinking at the scene before her. "Beth, who is this? I thought you, uh, didn't get picked?" I cast a questioning look at the man who held her possessively at his side. A low growl rumbled from the stranger's throat.

"Athena, this is Tyler," Beth explained, rolling her eyes at his possessiveness. "My, uh, second mate."

"Kinda?" Tyler interjected, looking confused.

"Okay, okay, my second-chance mate," Beth clarified with a sigh.

"Spill the details," I demanded, already intrigued by this unexpected turn of events. So, Beth launched into the story of how she followed Tyler's scent after the ceremony, ending up in his room and promptly spilling the beans about Alpha Mac.

"I'm guessing that didn't go over well?" I chuckled, picturing the aftermath.

Beth shook her head, a ghost of a smile playing on her lips. "The bathroom underwent some...unexpected renovations."

Tyler, clearly offended, puffed out his chest. "Well, could you blame me?"

"Alright, alright," I said, waving a hand dismissively. "He's on probation. If he treats you well, then he can stay."

Tyler's bravado instantly melted into a look of sheer terror. "D-don't worry, Luna, I would never..."

"Call me Athena," I interrupted. "Still getting used to the whole Luna thing."

With that, I scooped up a bewildered Midnight and headed back to our room. Finding Hayden sprawled asleep on the bed, I asked, "Did you release him?"

He mumbled a groggy "yeah" without moving.

"Good," I replied, setting Midnight down and closing the door. Crawling into bed, I pulled out my laptop.

"What are you doing?" Hayden mumbled through the sheets.

"Facetiming my grandparents. Haven't talked to them in a while." I clicked the call button and waited for them to answer.

The screen flickered to life, revealing my grandma's concerned face. "Honey, it's about time you called! We were starting to worry."

"Hey grandma, I'm fine. You know me, always causing trouble." Midnight nestled comfortably beside me as I spoke.

"Well, we have some news," my grandpa's voice boomed from the speaker.

"News? What kind of news?" I braced myself, a bad feeling creeping into my gut.

"The council wants to see you," my grandma explained. "They're curious about your mate."

My blood ran cold. "Wait, what?! Grandma, do you remember the last time I dealt with the council? That whole Damon thing didn't exactly go smoothly, and I still have the scar to prove it!"

Hayden gave me a confused look but I ignored him.

"I know sweetie but they want to know if having a werewolf mate will get in the way of your… hunting." She explained.

I sighed. "When do they want to see me?"

"As soon as you can." My grandpa answered.

"I'll see when I have time. Bye."

"Bye."

I clicked the red button ending the call.

I set my laptop down on the small table beside the couch.

"What council?" Hayden asked.

"You think supernatural creatures are the only ones with a council?"

"That's what I thought."

"Well, you thought wrong. Hunter has a council too. The council decides the laws for hunting supernatural creatures. They have been kept a secret for as long as werewolves have been hidden. For instance, werewolf hunters can only kill rogues but if a wolf from a pack attacks first then you can kill them." I explained.

"OK continue."

"Usually the council only summons you when you have broken a law. Other times they want to see you because of something that has happened during hunting. Example: Damon secretly being a rogue. If you break a major law then they will either retire early or become a rogue hunter."

"Rogue hunter?"

"You think werewolves are the ones who came up with the meaning of rogue?" I questioned.

"Sorry, please explain."

"Working as a rogue hunter without the council's authorization is a crime. They kill any werewolf in sight. They kill for fun. Some hunters are assigned to capture the rogue hunters and bring them to the council for punishment."

"So how did you become a hunter?"

"To become an official to the council you have to prove that you will follow the laws. I proved myself by killing Damon." I whispered the last part.

"It makes sense now," Hayden whispered.

"What does?" I asked.

"My mom, dad, and twin sister were killed by a rogue hunter."

"Hayden you don't have to tell me if you don't want to."

"I want to."

I nodded for him to continue.

"Me and my twin sister, Ash, shared a room when we were 9 years old. Every night my parents would come into our room and tell us stories. One night a person burst through the window. It was a hunter. He had a blade and killed my parents and sister. He was about to kill me until another hunter came in and killed him. The pack doctor said that my mom was pregnant with my baby brother. The hunter stabbed her stomach."

He broke down in tears.

I pulled him into a hug as he cried into my shoulder. "I'm so sorry that happened to you." I pulled him closer.

"It wasn't your fault. I'm just glad you're not like them." He kissed my lips.

I pulled away. "You should get some rest."

He nodded and got under the covers.

He pulled me closer and nuzzled his head in my neck.

"I love you Athena."

"I love you too."

CHAPTER NINETEEN

~Athena~

"Athena, wake up!" A voice, like Hayden's, pierced the silence. I ignored it, groaning and rolling over.

Another voice, similar to Robert's, chimed in, "Come on, Athena, you gotta get up."

I burrowed deeper into the pillow. Something cold slapped me in the face. Wiping it away with the blanket, I attempted to return to sleep.

"Seriously?! How is she still asleep?" Xavier's voice boomed. "We dumped a whole bucket of ice water on her!"

"Don't mess with a girl's beauty sleep," Jamie countered. "Yes!" Beth echoed.

Cracking open one eye, I saw Xavier holding a bucket, Robert and Hayden staring wide-eyed. Summer, Beth, and Jamie wore triumphant smirks.

My hair and clothes were inexplicably soaked. "Hey," I yawned. "What'd I miss? And why do I look like I just escaped a water park?"

Xavier sputtered, "You're serious? We threw water on you, and you wouldn't wake up!"

"Rude," I glared. "I never bother you when you're sleeping."

"How did you sleep through that?" Robert gaped.

"That bucket was a walk in the park compared to the cacophony of a five-year-old's birthday bash. Child's play," I declared.

They looked at me with a mix of awe and concern. "Anyway," I scowled, "why the wake-up call?"

"There's something wrong with Midnight," Hayden explained. "We've heard ten minutes of constant barking and howling from Midnight in the closet."

Faint whimpers reached my ears. Xavier continued, "We try to get close, and she growls and snaps."

"Sounds like Midnight," I admitted. "But why assume a problem? Maybe she's just... yowling?"

"Her howls sound like she's in pain," Robert countered.

Rising from the bed, I cautiously approached the closet door. Midnight huddled in the corner, whimpering and letting out pained howls.

"Calm down, girl," I soothed, walking slowly toward her.

Extending a hand to pet her head, I was met with a growl. Retracting my hand, I stepped back.

"Whoa, Midnight," I said, surprised. "You've never growled at me before."

She continued whimpering and howling. Turning to the others, I stated, "There's something wrong. She never growls at me."

Summer suggested, "Maybe the pack doctor? We're part canine, Midnight's full-on. Maybe it's a difference?"

Nodding, I agreed. "Someone has to take her, even if she fights us the whole way."

"I'll do it," Hayden volunteered.

He cautiously approached Midnight. She growled and snapped, but Hayden managed to pick her up, despite her grumbles.

We all headed to the pack doctor, placing Midnight on the examination table while Dr. Linda began her checkup.

"Luna," Dr. Linda smiled, "your dog is pregnant. She's giving birth."

"What?!" I exclaimed. "Alright, who mated with my dog?"

We all slowly turned to Xavier, who stammered, "Well, I might have taken her on a walk, and the leash might have slipped... and she might have been gone for a few hours. When I found her, she might have been with a German Shepherd." He heavily emphasized each "might."

"Xavier, you might be responsible for getting my dog pregnant!" I shouted, emphasizing the word 'might'.

With a sheepish grin and palms facing outwards, he conceded, "Look, I think it could be a good thing."

My glare intensified as I narrowed my eyes at him.

"Why that look?" Xavier stammered a tremor of fear in his voice.

With a tight smile, I said, "Planning a murder out loud? Not exactly your brightest moment, Xavier."

Xavier flinched back in fear.

"Athena, calm down," Hayden soothed, grabbing my hand.

"No," I resisted. "Lots of dogs don't make it after giving birth. What if that happens to Midnight?" My voice wavered.

He pulled me into a comforting hug. "Everything will be okay. Most dogs pull through just fine. We just need to let her deliver the pups."

"I can't lose her, Hayden. She's my best friend," I choked out, my voice breaking.

"Thanks for the appreciation," Xavier muttered sarcastically.

We all shot him a glare.

Knowing he'd messed up, Xavier mumbled a quick "Sorry, bad timing" and looked down at his feet.

"Luna, I can deliver the puppies, but everyone else needs to leave," Linda insisted.

"Are you sure you can handle this? You're a pack doctor, not a veterinarian," I questioned.

She gave a confident nod. "Positive."

With a sigh, I conceded, "Alright everyone, let's go." We left the room and settled into some uncomfortable chairs. Who designed these things, anyway?

The wait seemed endless until Linda returned, a smile on her face.

"Congratulations! Midnight successfully delivered six healthy puppies!"

I rushed to Midnight's side. She was peacefully nursing her six newborn pups.

"Can I keep one?" Xavier pleaded.

"No," I replied firmly.

He pouted. "Aw, come on. They're adorable! I was going to name that brown one Oatmeal."

"You can name them, but you can't keep any," I explained. "Besides, there are two brown ones."

"Yeah, but the other one has white paws. The Oatmeal-to-be doesn't," he clarified, pointing.

"Well, since Xavier already claimed Oatmeal, what other names are on the table?" I asked the group.

Ideas flew back and forth: Coco for the other brown one, Lucky for the brown and white, Stripes for the dark brown and white, Dip for the other dark brown with white (because of his "white-dipped" tail according to Jamie), and Clumsy for the final all-black pup who kept falling on its back.

Xavier interjected with a suggestion for the black pup just as I was about to agree on Clumsy.

"Wait a minute," Xavier interrupted, blurting out, "He kind of resembles that German Shepherd I saw with Midnight."

My glare silenced him immediately. "Just zip it."

Ignoring Xavier, I watched the clumsy pup struggle to right itself again.

"Clumsy it is then," I decided. "Looks like it fits him perfectly."

Everyone turned to see him on his back once more. Even Xavier shrugged in agreement.

"Now, how do we get this whole puppy crew back to the pack house?" Robert pondered.

"Box," Xavier offered simply.

"Beats a bedpan, I guess," I conceded with a shrug. Hayden materialized with a giant box. Working together, Robert carefully placed Midnight inside while Xavier added the wiggling puppies.

We made our way back to the pack house, Midnight fast asleep in the box. We settled her comfortably in the guest bedroom next to ours, still trying to process the fact that Xavier, of all people, got my dog pregnant.

CHAPTER TWENTY

~Athena~

It's been about two weeks and the puppies have grown a little bit. Midnight's still super protective, though. Xavier almost lost a digit trying to hold one – gotta love that werewolf healing, right?

They're mostly crawling around, but they're figuring out who gets the slow-and-steady approach. Some have cracked open their eyes, while others are still chilling in darkness.

'Athena, did you hear me?' Beth snapped me out of puppy-watching mode.

'Huh? No, Xavier was at it again, trying to pick up a pup.' I pointed towards him.

'Ow! Come on, Midnight!' he whined.

'Give them a break,' Summer chimed in. 'They're not exactly fans of yours.'

'Correction, Midnight hates me,' Xavier clarified. 'The jury's still out on the pups.'

'My verdict is already in,' Jamie cut in, making me snort with laughter. Xavier shot all of us a glare.

'Aw, babe, don't pout,' Summer cooed, rubbing his arm. He managed a smile. 'Be mad 'cause I'm teasing you too.'

Xavier grabbed Summer's waist, pulling her close as his eyes shifted color. 'You're tempting punishment, mate,' he smirked, making Summer blush.

'Maybe not the best idea, Jack,' Summer whispered. Jack must be his wolf's name.

'Oh, but I want to,' he countered, smirk still in place. 'Want to make you feel like a queen.'

'Wow, Xavier's wolf is the total opposite,' I pointed out. 'Charming and smooth.'

He glared in my direction before whispering something in Summer's ear that sent more blush creeping up her neck.

'Hey, lovebirds,' I cut in. 'Kitchen's for eating, not, well, whatever you two were planning.' Beth and Jamie snickered at my comment.

Xavier's eyes switched back to normal as he blushed too. I tried my hardest not to burst out laughing.

'Anyway, back to what I was saying,' Beth started. 'Shopping trip? Since it's my birthday today!'

'Your birthday?!' Summer, Jamie, and Xavier all yelled at once.

'Not a big birthday person,' I admitted.

'Why not?' Summer asked.

I sighed, leaning my forehead against the counter. 'It's the anniversary of my parents passing. Stopped celebrating birthdays after that.'

'Oh, Athena, I'm so sorry,' Beth apologized.

'It's okay. Let's just get out of here before I get all gloomy.'

'Sounds good,' Jamie agreed.

We piled into Jamie's car and started blasting Alessia Cara songs. Those girls are obsessed.

~Xavier~

"Athena's birthday? How come she never mentioned it?

Makes sense she wouldn't want a celebration, but still. We could have at least done something small.

'Maybe some fun with our mate,' Jack, my wolf, chimed in with a smirk.

'Always about getting laid, aren't you?' I asked him.

'Hey, it's not my fault Summer's heat is coming soon. Same thing for our Luna.'

'And you didn't tell me?!'

'You never asked.'

Fuming, I marched to Hayden's office and knocked on the door.

"Come in," he called out.

Opening the door, I plastered a fake-enthusiastic smile on my face. He was at his desk, buried in paperwork.

"Alright, so I have both good news and bad news. Which do you want first?" I asked.

"Bad news," he replied.

With a playful jab, I said, "Good news first, like it or not." His expression hardened into a glare.

"The good news is, it's Athena's birthday!"

He cracked a smile. "That's fantastic!"

"The bad news is the girls are going into heat soon."

His smile vanished. "What did you just say?"

"I said, 'The bad news is the girls are—'"

"I heard you the first time!" he yelled.

I puffed out my cheeks. "Rude," I muttered under my breath.

"What are we going to do?! They just went shopping. Who knows when they'll be back?"
"They can handle themselves, you know."
"Your mate is with them, right?!"
"Yeah, but they have Athena."
He growled. "Just get them back here ASAP."
"They just left, literally. Can't they have a little fun?"
"Alright, alright. Get your guards. But make sure it's at least five, and tell them to be discreet."
"Alright, sounds fair."

~Hayden~

Athena is going into heat. Hopefully, this doesn't cause a rift between us.
'Why would she hate us? She's practically begging to mate with us, right?' Jordan smirked.
'Cocky much?' I scoffed. 'No, not at all. Just stating facts.'
Rolling my eyes, I tuned him out.
A few hours later, Athena stormed into my office.
'I don't appreciate the private army you sent to babysit us,' she glared, marching towards me.
I pulled her onto my lap, wrapping my arms possessively around her waist. 'I had to.'
'I'm not a child, Hayden, and you can't keep smothering me.' She crossed her arms defiantly.
'But you're my baby,' I mumbled, nuzzling my face into the crook of her neck.
'And even your babies deserve some space.'

'Not when unmated males are lurking around.' I peppered kisses on her neck.

'Okay, seriously, the possessiveness is getting out of hand. What's going on?'

Ignoring her question, I trailed kisses down her neck, a smirk spreading across my face as she shivered in response.

Grabbing her hands, I gently guided them around my neck, ready to attack her neck with kisses again.

'Seriously, Hayden, spill it.'

Sighing, I finally confessed, 'You're going into heat soon.'

She groaned, burying her head in my chest. 'Again?!'

Pulling her closer, I consoled her. 'Why do females have to deal with this? Why not the males?' she pouted.

Sealing her pouty lip between my teeth, I kissed her deeply. Licking her lip for entrance, she denied me playfully. With a chuckle, I poked her sides, eliciting a surprised gasp. Taking advantage, I slipped my tongue into her mouth.

Pulling away, she glared. 'Brat.'

My jaw dropped playfully. 'Not enough tongue?' I smirked.

She shot me a fire-filled glare before playfully hitting my chest. 'Too much, you asshat.'

Chuckling, I braced myself for her next outburst, but instead, a scream ripped from her throat.

'My body is burning,' she gasped. 'It's like my skin is lava and I'm a volcano about to erupt!'

'Heat's got you, Princess.'

'It made me scream! I haven't screamed in years.' Another scream punctuated her sentence. 'Get rid of it!'

"Mating is the only way to ease the heat." And I can't do that unless you're ready.'

'Just do it!'

'In my office?!' I exclaimed.

Her eyes narrowed as she panted heavily. 'In the damn bedroom, you idiot!'

Grinning, I scooped her up bridal style and bolted for our bedroom. Slamming the door shut and locking it, I laid her gently on the bed. Hovering above her, I asked, one last time, 'Are you sure?'

She met my gaze with a determined nod.

Our kiss ignited, hers slow and searching, mine passionate and possessive."

CHAPTER TWENTY-ONE

~Athena~

I drifted off to sleep until a poking sensation jolted me awake. I swatted the hand away from my side.

The hand returned, this time exploring my stomach. I shot up and smacked it away, finding a chuckling Hayden beside me.

"There are better ways to wake me up, you know," I pointed out.

"Like what?" he challenged.

I grinned. "Shouting 'chocolate chip pancakes!' making them for me, then watching me fall back asleep."

"Only if I get to cuddle you while you snooze," Hayden said, pulling me close.

"Seriously? Still horny?" I teased.

"Always," he admitted with a wink.

He leaned in for a kiss, but the moment was interrupted by the ping of my laptop.

"Blast it! My grandparents are video calling," I groaned.

I grabbed my sports bra and threw on a shirt before setting the laptop on my lap and answering the call.

"Hi Grandma," I greeted.

"Who's shirt are you wearing?" she inquired, clearly noticing the oversized tee.

I glanced down – oops, Hayden's shirt it was. I shot him a glare as he tried (and failed) to contain his laughter.

"No one's, I just like baggy clothes," I lied unconvincingly. They're just so comfy!

"Alright, well, that aside, the council is getting impatient. They need to see you in three days."

"Three days? It takes four just to be safe for us to leave the pack!" I protested.

"I hear you, But a meeting with them is crucial, and they want to see both of you."

"Grandma, we can't just abandon our responsibilities here.

"But if an attack is imminent, we have to act."

My frustration mounted. I gripped my keys tightly. "Fine, Expect us in two hours."

"Alright, see you then, sweetie."

I slammed the laptop shut and tossed it on the side table.

With purposeful strides, I marched to the closet and grabbed clothes – jeans and a T-shirt.

As I headed to the bathroom, Hayden's arms wrapped around me.

"Athena, are you sure about this?" he asked.

I turned to him. "There's no choice. The council will attack if I don't go."

"Then I'm coming with you. They want to see me too, right?" He groaned.

"Yes, now get ready," I said, pushing him playfully.

I showered quickly and changed, then packed clothes for both of us. Who knows how long this council visit will take?

Heading downstairs to the living room, I found Xavier looking clueless. Robert stared at him in amusement.

Hayden sighed and rubbed his face. "Xavier, it's simple. You watch the pack for a while."

"Easy enough," Xavier said with a nod.

I couldn't resist a jab. "Just like your attention span."

He narrowed his eyes at me.

Hayden instructed Robert, "You watch Midnight and the pups too."

Xavier's face fell as he crossed his arms. "No fair!"

Midnight sashayed over to me and I scooped her up.

"Looking a little squishy after those pups, Midnight?" I teased.

She glared and barked back.

"Don't worry, it's just the council," I reassured her, setting her down with the puppies. "Robert, keep Xavier away from them, alright?"

Xavier flashed a thumbs-up while glaring at me.

"Seriously?" Xavier grumbled.

I checked my phone. "Hayden, we gotta hit the road."

"Alright, let me get the guards."

"Hold on," I stopped him.

"Why not?" he questioned.

"The council keeps a tight lid on their existence, limiting knowledge of them among werewolves. You're the first werewolf they've ever invited."

He sighed. "Safe? Are we sure about this?"

"Over a hundred elite hunters guarding the place. We'll be fine."

"Alright, let's go then."

"One more thing. I'm driving."

Xavier snorted. "You? Drive? I haven't even seen you on a bicycle."

I rolled my eyes, ignoring him. "My truck. We're taking it."

Hayden groaned. "Why the truck?"

"Because only I know where this council is hidden. It's a few hours' drive."

"But Athena, you'll be exhausted."

"I pulled an all-nighter, 36 hours straight, cracking a rogue case rumored to be council-connected. A few hours behind the wheel is a breeze."

Hayden sighed in defeat. "Alright, let's do this."

Hayden loaded the bags in the back and hopped into the passenger seat.

I slid into the driver's seat and pulled out of the driveway.

After a few hours on the road, I saw the massive gates ahead.

Hayden was thankfully asleep. Silver would overwhelm him for sure.

He started mumbling and stirring in his sleep before finally cracking open his eyes.

Uh oh.

"Silver? I smell silver!" he panicked.

I slammed on the brakes, stopping right in front of the gates.

"Calm down," I said, placing a hand on his arm. "Freak out, and they'll kill you."

He took a shaky breath and nodded, calming slightly.

A hunter approached the truck and tapped on my window. I rolled it down.

"Code?" he asked.

I sighed. "Robin Hood the Second."

His eyes widened briefly, but he recovered quickly.

I rolled the window up as he signaled the other hunters to open the gates.

"Second?" Hayden mumbled.

"Don't worry about it," I said simply, pulling back onto the road.

The mansion loomed ahead, a testament to the council's wealth, some might say showiness.

A guard took our bags and led us to our room.

Hayden flopped onto the bed like a deadweight.

"Tired already? I was the one behind the wheel all day," I teased him playfully.

"Yeah, those truck seats leave a lot to be desired in terms of comfort," he mumbled in response.

A smile played on my lips as I crawled in next to him on the bed.

He reached out and pulled me close, his body hovering protectively above mine.

"What are you up to?" I asked with a hint of amusement, even though I knew perfectly well what he had in mind.

"No idea what you're talking about," he smirked, trailing kisses down my neck, careful not to put his full weight on me.

"Oh really? Because this sure looks like something."

"Nope, nothing happening here at all," he insisted, before kissing my lips softly.

He pinned my wrists down on either side of my head, then pulled away.

"Actually, you know what? Maybe I'm not that tired after all."

CHAPTER TWENTY-TWO

~Hayden~

"Days of arguments between Athena and the council have me stuck here. I begged to join her, but the council wasn't ready to see me. Late nights and early mornings are her new routine. Hoping things don't explode, I plopped on the bed, restlessness gnawing at me. Time to find her, I guess.

Out the door I went, wandering the halls until a girl sidled up. 'New face,' she smirked, running a finger down my chest. 'Cute too.' I stopped her hand. 'Appreciate it, but I'm taken.'

A sly look crossed her face. 'Never stopped me before.'

'Hands off,' Athena materialized beside me, glaring daggers.

'I like the possessiveness,' Jordan snickered in my head. 'Do too for once,' I silently agreed.

Athena turned on the girl. 'Some clothes, Blondie. This ain't a peep show.' Stifling laughter was a struggle, especially with Jordan's full-blown amusement in my head.

'Code?' the girl demanded, crossing her arms. Asking for code names instead of names is, the cool system they have here for hunters.

'Robin Hood the Second,' Athena replied. Why 'second,' I always ask. A kiss is her usual way of deflecting. Not complaining, but curious nonetheless.

The girl's eyes widened before a smirk returned. 'Her daughter, huh? Your mom's legacy, big shoes to fill.' With that, she sauntered off, leaving Athena fuming.

I wrapped my arms around her from behind. 'Love the possessiveness,' I whispered in her ear, a smirk playing on my lips.

'Hush. Why are you even out here?' she snapped.
'Got bored. Came looking for you. Your excuse?'
'Five-minute break.'
'Can I join yet?'
'Nope. Not yet. Back to the room.' She started walking again, and this time, I stuck by her side."

~Athena~

"For the last time Athena! It is not safe for you and your mate to be together!" One of the members of the council yelled.

Fury clenched my hand around the podium.

'We can't be sure of that!' another countered. 'I believe they'll be alright.'

'The risk is too high,' a third voice chimed in.

'Maybe it's not!' the first one argued back.

Their voices overlapped in a cacophony of disagreement. I slammed my fist on the podium with all my might, silencing them instantly. Every head snapped towards me, mouths agape.

'With all due respect,' I began, my voice steely, 'when was the last time this council made a wise choice?'

Their surprise was evident. 'You took on your mother's legacy with our blessing,' one stammered. "You assured me Damon was safe, though he never received a proper DNA test. Now I can't be with my mate?' I roared.

Silence hung heavy in the air.

'The council hasn't made a single good call since I became a hunter,' I pressed. 'And I doubt this will be any different.'

One member finally spoke, 'Your mother had a werewolf mate as well. However, your human DNA overpowers the wolf, making you not a true werewolf. That's why being with your mate is so dangerous. Letting your wolf side control you could easily kill everyone here.'

'That's exactly the problem!' I retorted. 'You're scared of what might happen if I stay with my mate!'

With that, I stormed out, fury fueling my every step until I reached our room. The door hung slightly ajar. I cautiously nudged it open to reveal Hayden engrossed in a book.

'Since when did you become a bookworm?' I inquired, shutting and locking the door behind me.

'Just started,' he replied, a touch too quickly.

'Why was the door open?' I pressed.

'Honestly, no clue,' he feigned ignorance.

'Don't lie to me,' I warned.

'Fine, you got me,' he conceded. 'I was worried sick since you'd been gone so long.'

'This picture,' he said, pulling out a frame. 'Is you?'

It held an image of a woman in hunter's attire, mirroring my black hair, green eyes, bow and quiver, and even the familiar gold coin.

'One problem,' I said, snatching the frame. 'That's not me.'

'Then who is it? It's your spitting image,' he said, utterly bewildered.

A sigh escaped my lips. 'You were eavesdropping on my council meeting, weren't you?'

'Alright, alright, you caught me,' he admitted. 'But only because your absence did make me worry."

'That woman in the picture is my mother,' I revealed. 'She was the original Robin Hood. I thought Damon gave me that name, but apparently, my grandparents told him about her. So, I'm not the original after all.'

I slumped down beside him. 'My mom had a werewolf mate, but the council doesn't want me with you because I'm half-werewolf. They're terrified of what might happen if we're together.'

A growl rumbled deep in his chest at the thought of separation.

He towered over me. 'They won't break us apart. No one!' His lips slammed onto mine in a possessive kiss.

I tangled my fingers in his hair, tugging playfully. He groaned in response, a sound of approval.

Reluctantly, I pulled away. 'No one will take me away,' I promised.

His smile widened before claiming my lips again, this time his tongue demanding entrance. I playfully blocked him.

'Stop teasing me,' he grumbled.

'Where's the fun in that?' I countered with a mischievous grin.

He playfully glared at me before once more capturing my lips, his tongue finding its way into my mouth. A moan escaped my lips, and I could feel the smirk against my skin.

His hand slid under my shirt, inching towards my skin, but a sharp rap on the door interrupted him. He growled, but I silenced him with a quick slap to the head. He glared at me, rubbing the spot I hit.

'Athena King!' a voice called from beyond the door. 'The council has reached a decision. They request your presence and your mate's immediately.'

'Thank you,' I replied. 'We'll be there shortly.'

My gaze met Hayden's. 'Ready to meet the council?'"

CHAPTER TWENTY-THREE

~Athena~

Hand-in-hand with Hayden, we reached the council chambers. A reassuring squeeze from him as we entered the room filled with stern faces, their gazes fixated on our intertwined fingers. We walked towards the podium, keeping our eyes down.

A booming voice declared the council's decision. A flicker of hope passed between Hayden and me.

The voice paused, building the tension, before finally announcing permission for us to be together. Relief and joy flooded me as a wide grin spread across my face.

"The Moon Goddess brought you together for a reason," another voice stated, granting us the freedom to leave whenever we wished.

Unable to hold back my excitement, I pulled Hayden into a tight embrace, followed by a passionate kiss.

"Homeward abound," Hayden beamed, his eyes sparkling with happiness. I nodded enthusiastically.

••••

Back at the pack house, the guards took our bags as we entered the darkened space – windows covered, lights out.

"Hello?" I called out cautiously.

A sudden burst of light revealed a welcoming committee: Summer, Jamie, Beth, Justin, Johnny, Robert, and Xavier. Blinking away the sudden brightness, we were greeted by a chorus of cheers. Xavier, sporting a red and white striped shirt and an adult diaper, sat regally on a tricycle in the center of the room. I stifled a laugh, while Hayden mirrored my struggle with amusement.

"Xavier," I managed, "did you just graduate from diaper duty?" I joked lightly.

He scowled. "Lost a bet, alright?"

"Bet you wouldn't wear it?" I teased, finally letting out a laugh.

Justin chimed in, explaining the bet was whether Xavier could teach a puppy to skateboard.

"Winner, Justin?"

He smirked and gave a thumbs-up.

Summer inquired hopefully about the council's decision.

"My guess," Xavier piped up smugly, "is they said you two are good to go," I confirmed his guess with a nod.

"Sharp as ever," Hayden acknowledged.

"Takes one to know one," Xavier retorted, earning another playful glare from me.

"Where's Midnight?" I asked, changing the subject.

As if on cue, Midnight bounded in, barking excitedly as she jumped into my arms.

"Missed you, girl?" I asked, her enthusiastic barks a clear answer.

Hayden offered his hand, but Midnight only whined and tilted her head in a noncommittal way.

"Maybe another time," I offered, putting her down.

"Back to normalcy, everyone," I announced. "But hey," Beth interrupted, pointing towards the kitchen, "we made barbecue!"

"Food!" I exclaimed, already rushing towards the delicious aroma.

We spent the next few hours talking, devouring food, and playing with the energetic puppies. I even confided in them about my mom and dad. Though surprised by my half-werewolf heritage, they were accepting and happy I shared my secret.

Duty called for Hayden, and he reluctantly left to fulfill missed pack meetings. With the urge to connect with my grandparents, I retreated to our room upstairs. Grabbing my laptop, I initiated a call – it had been a while since we last spoke.

Silence. No answer. This was unusual; they always picked up. Shrugging it off, I decided a walk was in order. Hunting rogues had fallen by the wayside lately.

After donning my hunter's attire, I ventured into the forest. A glint of light caught my eye, nestled amongst the trees. With cautious steps, I approached the source.

It was an envelope, adorned with a familiar gold coin. My heart pounded as I picked it up and read the chilling message:

"Are you missing something, Athena? I believe you are. Hank and Linda are now with me. Don't even think about getting them back easily. Another note will follow soon. And keep this little secret from your

boyfriend, or they might just meet an unnatural end.
~Damon"

Tears welled up in my eyes. Damon had taken my grandparents! I had no choice but to follow his twisted demands, I couldn't lose them.

The gold coin attached to the note belonged to my grandma - a women-and-gold-coin thing in my family, I guess. Wiping away tears, I hurried back to the pack house.

'Athena, are you alright?' Hayden's voice echoed in my mind through the mind link.

'Yeah, everything's fine. Nothing to worry about,' I replied, forcing a cheerful tone.

"I'll be back soon, alright? Just needed to see you're okay for me."

"Alright, see you soon. Just dropping by to make sure you're okay."

'Alright, love you.'

'Love you too.'

Severing the mind link, I re-entered the pack house. A second note, identical to the first, lay on the bed beside another matching envelope.

Locking the door behind me, I nervously opened it. This time, it wasn't a letter, but horrific pictures. My grandparents, battered and bruised, stared back at me. Cuts marred their bodies. A wave of guilt crashed over me, and tears streamed down my face. I couldn't escape the feeling that this was all my fault.

After wiping them away, I hid the photos and notes deep within the closet. Telling Hayden was out of the question, not if it meant endangering my grandparents' lives.

A warm shower and a change into PJs offered a temporary escape. A knock on the door startled me. Opening it revealed a weary Hayden, dark circles under his eyes, on the verge of collapse.

Without a word, I wrapped my arm around his waist, the other around his shoulder, guiding him towards the bed.

"Rough day?" I inquired, settling him down gently.

"Thanks for the observation," he mumbled sarcastically.

Glaring playfully, I lay down beside him. He nuzzled his head against my shoulder, pulling me closer.

"Four meetings, mountains of paperwork, and training the guards – that's my excuse for looking like a zombie," he mumbled against my ear.

"Get some sleep," I whispered back. "It's payback time! You've had your share of worrying, now let me take care of you."

He simply nodded and drifted off to sleep. Me? Sleep was a distant dream, haunted by the knowledge of my grandparents' peril.

CHAPTER TWENTY-FOUR

~Athena~

It's been two days, and still no sign of another note from Damon. My nerves are on edge lately. Even the smallest things make me jump a mile high.

Suddenly, a tap on my shoulder. I practically launched myself across the kitchen, flinging a sizzling piece of bacon right at the culprit's face.

"Ow! Athena, what the heck was that?!" Xavier yelped, dropping the bacon to the floor with a splat. His face was a greasy mess. Midnight's pups materialized in seconds, happily devouring the fallen bacon.

"Xavier! You scared the living daylights out of me!" I shouted.

"Yeah, kinda obvious," he mumbled, wiping the grease off his face with his hands.

"Great, just a waste of perfectly good bacon," I sighed, pointing at the puppies.

"What's gotten into you? You've been jumpy all week." Xavier inquired.

"Nothing. I'm fine," I lied unconvincingly.

"Uh-huh. Sure you are." He gave a noncommittal grunt, followed by a skeptical arch of his eyebrow.

"Just drop it, alright?" I snapped, slamming the pan back on the stove and storming out of the kitchen.

Upstairs in mine and Hayden's room (he was at a meeting), I found another note waiting for me on the bed. My heart hammered in my chest as I picked it up and slowly unfolded it.

"Good choice. You obeyed. Over the years I've known you (creepy much?), I know you'd do anything for your family. Meet me in the forest tonight at midnight. Don't even think about pulling anything funny, and come dressed as Robin Hood. ~Damon"

Ugh. I had to go. He was right, I would do anything for my grandparents.

Folding the note back up, I hid it with the others in the corner of the closet. Just then, a knock on the door made me flinch. Taking a deep breath, I opened the door to find Summer, Jamie, and Beth standing there.

"Hey guys, what's up?" I asked, surprised.

"We were thinking, how about a girls' day out?" Jamie suggested.

"Yeah, sure! Sounds good. Where are we headed?" I replied, stepping aside to let them in.

"Food first, then a shopping spree!" Beth chimed in.

We piled into Summer's car and drove off.

"Steakhouse?" I chimed in already craving a juicy meal.

"Perfect!" Jamie and Beth agreed in unison.

The restaurant wasn't far, and we settled into a booth by the window. We all ordered medium-rare steaks with mashed potatoes and gravy – looks like we all had the same taste in food.

"How long does this food take anyway?" After only two minutes, Beth expressed her impatience with a grumble.

"It's been two minutes," Jamie pointed out.

"But that's forever when you're hungry!" Beth countered dramatically.

Just as the food arrived, Summer cleared her throat and announced with a huge grin, "I have some news, everyone!"

We all looked up, attention grabbed. "I'm pregnant!" she declared.

Our jaws dropped in unison.

"When?!" I exclaimed, genuinely happy for her.

"Just found out this morning! Xavier and I are gonna be parents!" Summer explained.

"Oh no," I gasped, though a smile tugged at my lips.

"What's wrong?" Jamie asked.

"Xavier, a parent? Their kid is doomed to be spoiled rotten," I joked.

We all dissolved into laughter.

The conversation flowed, filled with baby name suggestions. Summer's due date was still up in the air, somewhere between five and six months from now.

Forty-five minutes later, our food finally arrived. Just then, a face caught my eye outside the window. It was Damon, a smirk plastered across his face, staring intently at Jamie, Summer, and Beth.

"Hold on, everyone! Don't touch your steaks!" I exclaimed urgently, stopping them mid-bite.

Confused looks met mine as they lowered their forks. I snatched Beth's steak and swiftly cut it in half.

"Hey!" she protested.

Ignoring her outburst, I pried open the meat. The center was a disturbing shade of red, dotted with pink. A pungent smell hit my nose. "Wolfsbane," I confirmed.

Gasps erupted around the table. I quickly wrapped the tainted steak in a bandana I always carried.

We exited the steak house in a hurry, piling back into Summer's car and heading straight for the pack house. Upon entering, we were met with a chorus of worried greetings from our mates. Even Tyler couldn't hide his concern for Beth.

"Where have you all been?!" Hayden roared, his voice laced with anger.

"We have bigger problems!" I countered, my voice sharp.

"Like what?" he demanded.

"Someone tried to poison us with wolfsbane!" Summer cried out. "And let me tell you, wolfsbane doesn't exactly pair well with steak!"

Xavier immediately pulled her into a protective embrace, followed by the others who rushed to comfort their mates.

"You didn't even tell me where you were going? What were you thinking?" Hayden directed his question at me.

"You never asked," I retorted, pulling away from the group hug.

"Athena, you're still part werewolf! Wolfsbane can affect you too," he pointed out, his tone laced with concern.

An eye roll escaped me. "Not yet."

I retrieved the tainted steak from my pocket and presented it to Hayden. "Someone laced our food with wolfsbane."

He took the steak, his nostrils flaring as he sniffed it. A low growl rumbled in his chest. "Take this to Owen, the pack scientist. Find out how they managed to inject this much wolfsbane into the meat," he commanded, his voice firm. Robert simply nodded in agreement.

Just then, Summer broke the tense silence with an unexpected announcement. "Well, now seems like a good time to tell everyone... I'm pregnant!"

A collective gasp filled the room. Xavier looked like he might faint any second.

"Xavier? Aren't you going to say something?" I questioned.

He seemed to ignore me, scooping Summer up in his arms and spinning her around with a goofy grin plastered on his face.

"Whoa there, big guy," Jamie chimed in. "You might hurt the baby if you squeeze her too tight."

Xavier carefully set Summer down, a nervous energy radiating from him.

Hayden, taking my hand, led me upstairs. I shuffled along behind him, feeling exhausted. We reached our room, and I slammed the door shut before locking it.

"You're still in trouble for leaving without telling me," he began.

"Hayden, stop it. I'm not a kid." I argued.

"I know, but you could've been hurt. Nobody would have known where to find you."

"Stop worrying so much," I scoffed. "I can handle myself."

"I care about you, Athena. I want to protect you."

He leaned in and kissed my lips, his touch sending shivers down my spine. Wrapping my arms around his neck, I deepened the kiss.

He pulled away reluctantly, his eyes locking with mine. "If I don't stop now," he murmured, his voice barely a whisper, "I won't be able to control myself."

"Then don't stop," I whispered.

~Athena's Dream

Darkness. Absolute darkness. I couldn't see a thing.

All I could do was wander, hoping nothing would brush against my face in the inky blackness.

Suddenly, a blinding light erupted. I blinked repeatedly, adjusting to the sudden brightness.

Standing before me was a couple – the same couple from my baby picture.

"Mommy? Daddy?" I cried, rushing towards them and pulling them into a hug.

"My little girl, all grown up," my mom's voice filled my ears.

"What are you doing? I mean, it's amazing to see you, of course!" I responded.

"We came to warn you about your werewolf side and Damon," my dad grumbled.

"What about them?"

"You possess the werewolf gene, but you won't be able to shift," my mom explained.

I nodded, urging them to continue.

"Damon seeks vengeance," my dad said. "You must outsmart him to defeat him. Don't let his words manipulate you."

"Okay, I won't," I confirmed, nodding firmly.

"Time to wake up, sweetheart. It's almost midnight," my mom said before they both vanished into thin air.

~End of Dream

I slowly opened my eyes and looked at the clock. 11: 42.

I slowly removed Hayden's arm from around my waist and got dressed as Robin Hood.

I quietly exited the house and ran into the dark forest.

CHAPTER TWENTY-FIVE

~Athena~

I was a long way from the pack's border. Trees, mountains, and rocks were all I could see.

'Hi!' A loud voice suddenly popped into my head.

'What the fu-' I started to swear but was cut off.

'No need to swear.'

'What and who are you?' I demanded.

'I'm your wolf, Jean.' She smiled.

'Oh, hi,' I greeted awkwardly.

'Anyway, why are you out here in the middle of nowhere?' she inquired.

'Look through my memories and you'll understand,' I replied, blocking her out.

I soon emerged into a clearing where a familiar face stood waiting, a smirk plastered across his face.

"You made the right decision, Athena," he said, smirk still in place.

"Before we negotiate, answer a question. How are you alive?" I demanded, clearly ticked off.

He feigned deep thought. "Well, you've waited long enough, I suppose."

I waited for him to elaborate.

"After you tried to kill me with silver, my wolf went berserk. It took everything he had to heal me, a huge toll that ended up killing him. But somehow, I could still shift. That's how I'm here, healthy and alive."

I stood there, devoid of emotion. I was frozen, unable to muster a single word in response.

'I barely know him and I can already tell I hate him,' Jean scowled in my mind.

Damon started speaking again. "I brought you here to take you back with me."

"That's hilarious. You still think you can take me?" I scowled back.

"Oh, I can't take you. But what you don't know is this is an ambush." He smirked with amusement.

On cue, a bunch of werewolves jumped down from the trees.

Oh no. I'd let my guard down, completely oblivious to their presence.

"You underestimate me, Damon. I've survived far deadlier attacks."

I pulled out my dagger, ready for a fight.

They all lunged at me at once. I managed to stab the ones in front, but the ones behind me grabbed and held me down.

Damon approached and held a rag to my mouth. I accidentally inhaled, and everything went black.

••••

My eyes fluttered open slowly. I took a quick scan of my surroundings. Disoriented, I realized I was trapped in the back of a moving vehicle.

No weapons. Anywhere.

A sign caught my eye: 'Johnson Warehouse' with spray paint obscuring some of the letters, spelling 'abandoned' underneath.

Suddenly, I was yanked out of the car with force. A blindfold was slapped on my face as someone dragged me somewhere.

The blindfold was ripped off moments later, and I was shoved into a cell. Someone chained my wrist to the wall.

It was Damon.

"Don't even think about mind-linking your mate. I had a witch put a spell around the warehouse to block any human-werewolf communication," he smirked.

"Oddly specific," I pointed out. "How many other human-werewolf couples have you trapped here?"

His smirk faltered. "Still the same smartass, I see."

"That's me."

"Whatever. I'll be back. Don't even try escaping."

"Wait! What did you do with my grandparents?" I stopped him.

"I let them go. The deal was that if you turn yourself in, they walk free. I always keep my promises, Athena." He slammed the cell door shut and left.

At least they're safe.

'So I've been through your memories and I have to say I hate that guy.' Jean said. 'But the memories with Hayden cheered me right up.'

I rolled my eyes at her. 'You better not be putting dirty thoughts in my head.'

'No promises.' She smirked. 'He's a Greek God. How do you not have dirty thoughts?'

I rolled my eyes at her again and blocked her out.

I could see some sort of shine peeking out from outside of my cell.

The sun is coming up. Hayden must have noticed I'm gone by now.

Hopefully, he doesn't come looking for me. I don't want him to risk his life for me.

Damon came back with a plate of food in his hands. He kneeled in front of me and held a spoon of old moldy peas to my mouth.

"Eat." He commanded.

I looked at him like he was crazy. "Why don't you eat that? Let's see if your stomach can hold that shit down."

"Athena you have to eat this food."

"Only one problem, that's not food. It's something you puke up after drinking too much."

He rolled his eyes at me. "If I take a bite will you eat it?"

"Maybe."

He sighed and brought the spoon to his mouth.

I waited for him to swallow so I could see the look on his face when he puked it up.

He swallows and smirks. His smirk falls when I hear his stomach grumbling.

"You know what never mind. Starve to death for all I care." He dropped the plate of food in front of me and left the cell.

I looked over at the plate. Is that cabbage? I hate cabbage.

'Why?' Jean asked.

'Cabbage is lettuce's snobby cousin.' I answered.

'Well, I can't argue with that logic.'

'No one can. It's only science.'

'Wait I just had an idea.' She paused for a few seconds.
'Well don't keep me in suspense. Tell me what it is.'
'The spell was only meant to stop humans from contacting their mates but we are half werewolf. The spell won't work on us.'
'That's perfect! Also, I forgot that I keep a dagger in my boot. We can escape and tell Hayden where we are.'
I blocked her out and mind-linked Hayden.
'Hayden? Hello?'
'Athena where are you!? I have been worried sick. Tell me where you are so I can come get you!' He yelled.
'Calm down! Damon kidnapped my grandparents so I turned myself over to him. I'm in Johnson's Warehouse.'
'Which one? There are over 50 warehouses!'
'An abandoned one, I don't know exactly which one but that's all I know.'
'Ok, I'm coming for you. Stay there.'
'Well, it's not like I can just walk out the front door!'
He blocked me out.
I noticed that the chains on my wrist were attached to loose parts of the wall.
If I use my werewolf strength I can escape and find Hayden.
I just have to wait for the right time.
Damon comes back with a pizza box in his hand.
I quickly stand up and pull on the chains until they're realized from the way along with a chunk of cement on them.

I pull on the chains on my wrist until they snap.

Damon just stands there shocked forgetting the open door.

I shove him into the cell while grabbing the pizza box. I took two slices and held them in my mouth while closing the cell door leaving a confused and angry Damon.

I eat the pieces of pizza while looking at where they put my weapons.

CHAPTER TWENTY-SIX

~Athena~

After what felt like an eternity of searching, I finally located my weapons!

"What are you doing here?!" a furious voice boomed from behind.

Spinning around, I came face-to-face with one of my kidnappers. Without hesitation, I tackled him to the ground, the glint of my recovered knife reflecting menacingly at his throat.

"My weapons?" I growled, emphasizing each word.

"Not a chance!" he snarled back.

"Let me rephrase," I said, tightening my grip on the blade. His bravado quickly faded, replaced by a widening of the eyes. "Fine," he choked out, "they're past the torture chamber, at the end of the cell block."

"Good boy," I muttered, before relieving him of his consciousness with a well-placed punch. That's right, one hit wonder over here.

Feeling a surge of power reminiscent of a certain caped crusader, I followed his directions. Reaching a sign marked "Torture Chamber," I cautiously bypassed it, thankfully devoid of screams. Ignoring the ominous "Do Not Enter" sign, I found my missing arsenal within. As always, breaking the rules pays off.

Snatching my equipment, I made a swift exit. Surprisingly, the path was clear, leading me straight to an escape route. The sun, a giant ball of fire in the sky, nearly blinded me with its brilliance. Blinking away the temporary blindness, I started walking, the familiar forest bordering the warehouse a reassuring landmark.

Reaching out with my mind, I called out to Hayden, "I'm back in the forest. Where are you?"

Silence. Fear started to gnaw at me. "Dammit, Hayden, answer me!" I yelled into the void. No response.

A glint in the distance caught my eye. Another note, tucked into a tree. With trepidation, I retrieved it.

The message sent a jolt through me:

"Is someone missing their big bad alpha? I snagged you to get to your little plaything. Don't worry, he's not alone. He's got company - your grandparents, his second-in-command, beta, their mates, some of your warriors and trackers. Don't even think about rescuing them, or they die.
~Damon"

Panic surged through me. "Hayden? Hayden! Answer me!" Tears streamed down my face. This is all my fault.

A desperate urge to save them warred with the terrifying knowledge that I'd only make things worse. "Find them!" Jean roared, seizing control.

"I can't, he'll kill them!" I argued back.

"You killed Damon before. Do it again!"

"Jean, I can't!" I pleaded.

"Then I will!" she snarled, a fierce struggle for dominance igniting within me.

A searing pain erupted in my head as she wrestled control. Instinctively, I raised my hands to my throbbing head.

"Jean, stop!" I cried out.

"No! I have to save my mate!" she countered, her voice a guttural growl.

My vision began to blur, colors swirling and shifting as our internal battle raged. My eyes changed completely. Jean was in control. I was powerless to intervene.

~Hayden~

I woke up to an empty bed.

I looked to the bathroom. It was empty.

"Athena?" I called out to the room.

'She's probably downstairs.' Jordan thought.

Without wasting a moment, I got dressed and dashed to the kitchen.

The only person that was there was Xavier.

"Have you seen Athena?" I ask.

He turned around to look at me. "No."

I kept a confused look on my face as I went back upstairs to mine and Athena's room.

I began to get worried.

Maybe she left a note.

I looked all around the room. No note.

Where is she!?

Something caught my eye in the corner of the closet.

It was letters from Damon. I growled as I read them.

Of course, Athena would go and get her grandparents!

She's too hard-headed and stubborn to let him go.

'The Luna is missing I want my best tracker to try and find her scent!' I mind-linked my warriors and trackers.

'Athena!? Are you ok?' I tried to mind-link her.

No answer.

I growled and punched the wall.

If he touches her I'm killing him on the spot.

'Hayden? Hello?' I heard Athena's voice in my head.

'Athena where are you!? I have been worried sick. Tell me where you are so I can come and get you.' I yelled.

'Calm down! Damon kidnapped my grandparents so I turned myself over to him. I'm in Johnson's warehouse.'

'Which one? There are over 50 wear houses!'

'An abandoned one. I don't know exactly which one but that's all I know.'

There are only two abandoned ones. Finding her should be easy.

'Ok, I'm coming for you. Stay there.' I commanded.

'Well, it's not like I can just walk out the front door!'

I ignored her sarcastic little comment and blocked her out.

'Even kidnapped she can turn me on with her sarcasm.' Jordan swooned.

'Not the time, Jordan.' I scowled.

I gathered up all of my trackers and worriers and headed to one of the abandoned wear houses.

We caught a small whiff of her scent in the woods but vanished.

We got to one of the wear houses.

I smelled her scent here. It was stronger than it was in the woods.

I was about to take a step closer to it but a man stopped me with a smirk on his face.

I growled. "Where's my mate, Damon!"

"Relax asshat. She's fine. Safely inside. Sadly."

I growled. "What is your problem with her!? Why did you take her!?"

"She killed my wolf! Why do you think I took her!? "She'll lose everything she holds dear!" he roared.

"You lied to her, and for that, you'll pay with your life when I touch you!"

"I don't think that's going to happen anytime soon." He smirked before snapping his fingers.

I heard small noises. I saw everyone behind me getting dizzy and holding and rubbing their necks.

After a few seconds, they started collapsing to the ground.

I had a confused look on my face before I felt a sharp pain on the side of my neck.

I groaned. I felt something sticking out of my neck. I pulled it out and stared at the blood, on my fingers, as my vision blurred.

It was a dart with wolfsbane in it. I tossed the dart, in a random direction, angrily.

I glared at Damon who was smirking as I started to see three of him.

I started getting dizzy and losing my balance but I refused to collapse.
I stood my ground as I stumbled backward a bit.
Damon snapped his fingers again before I felt more sharp pains in my neck in different areas.
I finally collapsed on the floor and glared at Damon with pure hatred.
He seemed amused at my reaction towards him.
He was enjoying seeing me in pain.
He walked over to me and kicked my face.
My vision blurred even more. Defiance burned in my eyes even as he delivered another blow to my face.
I love you Athena.
Then it all went black.

CHAPTER TWENTY-SEVEN

~Hayden~

A surge of pain lanced through my cheek, jolting me awake. My eyelids flew open just as Damon's backhand connected. "Took you long enough," he sneered. "Three days you've been out cold, snoring like a lumberjack."

I attempted to move, but a searing sting erupted from my wrist. Glancing around, I saw Xavier, Summer, Robert, Jamie, Beth, Tyler, Justin, and Johnny – all chained to the wall like captured beasts. Even Athena's grandparents were there, their faces grim. The silver glint of their restraints mocked any hope of escape.

I struggled again, the effort proving futile. "Don't bother," Damon drawled, boredom etched on his face. "Those are silver chains. They hold werewolves like you."

A growl rumbled in my chest, barely escaping my parched throat. "Disappointed, huh?" He rasped. "Don't flatter yourself. I couldn't care less."

"Too bad, because I'm telling you anyway," he smirked. I rolled my eyes as he launched into his monologue.

"What a shame. Your Luna seems to lack the courage to face me. A pity, I was hoping for a bit of a struggle. A worthy opponent would be a welcome change." He smirked and sauntered towards the cell door.

Shock washed over me. Athena wouldn't abandon us. It wasn't in her nature. She'd fight tooth and nail, strategize, find a way. If anyone, she'd be plotting our rescue right now.

"Hey, are we okay here?" I croaked out to the others.

"Peachy," Summer retorted sarcastically. "Chained to a wall with silver. What do you think?"

"I'm going to pretend it's just your hormones talking," I countered, a weak attempt at humor.

"Summer, calm down," Xavier interjected, his voice laced with worry.

"No! You heard the guards, right? Not a single sign of Athena or Robin Hood. She's not coming," Summer argued, her voice cracking with despair.

"The day Athena betrays her pack is the day pigs fly," Justin declared, earning him a bewildered look from Johnny.

"Well, she better start practicing then, because she's nowhere to be seen!" Jamie yelled, frustration boiling over.

"Why are you doubting her?" I snapped. "It hasn't even been that long!"

"Easy for you to say, Mr. Sleeping Beauty," Beth shot back before she could be cut off.

"Enough!" Athena's grandmother boomed, her voice echoing through the cell. We all flinched, surprised by the power radiating from her. "If I know my granddaughter, and trust me, I do, she'll be here. Now stop your bickering and conserve your strength!"

A collective nod of agreement rippled through the group.

"For a human, she's demanding," Xavier muttered under his breath, earning a glare from Summer.

The door creaked open again, revealing Damon and a woman dressed in a black outfit, a hockey mask obscuring her face. A deadly glint emanated from the sword strapped to her back. Her sharp black eyes scanned the room before settling on me.

"Meet Ninja," Damon announced with a smug grin. "My assassin, tasked with keeping you lovely folks in line. Human, but the best in the business, they say. They call her Ninja because she never speaks a word."

"Why wait around, Damon?" I rasped, the injustice of it all burning in my gut. "Just kill us and get it over with."

"Whoa there, Romeo," Beth hissed, her voice laced with fear. "Trying to get us all executed?"

Damon ignored her, kneeling before me. "The pain you feel now, she feels it too. I want her to suffer with you before I end your miserable lives." He smirked, rising to his feet. "Make sure they don't try anything funny," he barked at the masked figure before sauntering out.

The heavy metal door slammed shut, leaving us with our captor. Her gaze remained fixed on me, an unnerving intensity radiating from beneath the mask.

"What's the deal with the hockey mask?" Xavier drawled, attempting to lighten the mood. "Doesn't exactly scream 'assassin chic.'"

The woman's head snapped towards him in a flash, a silent warning.

"Xavier?" Summer scolded, shaking her head. "Do you have a death wish?"

The masked figure stalked towards him, her movements fluid and silent. Crouching before him, she leaned in close, and I could almost swear I saw a glint of amusement in her eyes.

With a swift movement, she rose to her feet and positioned herself in front of me.

"What do you want?" I spat.

She kneeled to my eye level and put her hand on the side of my face.

I flinched away when I felt a slight spark.

What the hell!?

"You're cute." She spoke up.

This is getting weird. That voice sounded familiar.

She took off her hockey mask. "I think I'll keep you."

"Athena?" My eyes widened.

A surge of electricity shot through me as her lips met mine. I responded instinctively, the kiss fueled by relief and a desperate longing.

She pulled away abruptly, a playful glint in her eyes. "Wrong guess, big guy."

Confusion clouded my features. "What do you mean wrong guess?"

"The name's Jean," she declared with a mischievous grin. "Athena's wolf at your service."

This revelation would send Jordan into a frenzy, I thought with a chuckle.

With practiced ease, she slipped the silver shackles from my wrists before repeating the process for everyone else. A joyous reunion unfolded as she embraced her grandparents, their relief palpable.

"Thank the heavens," Justin muttered under his breath. "I thought I might have to kiss Damon."

Athena, no, Jean (the habit would take some getting used to), chuckled and turned to him with a raised eyebrow. "What was that?"

"Nothing!" he squeaked, his cheeks flushing crimson.

Rolling her eyes playfully, she leaped into my arms, burying her face in my chest. I held her tight, the fear of losing her a fresh memory.

Pulling back slightly, I captured her lips in another heated kiss, the urgency of the situation momentarily forgotten. "Jean," I murmured against her mouth, "let Athena come back."

A slow nod followed as her emerald eyes flickered back into existence.

"No offense," Summer chimed in, "but what took you so long?"

"Needed a little backup," Athena replied, a hint of sheepishness in her voice as she stepped out of my embrace.

"Backup? And is that why you look like you raided a Halloween store?" Summer pressed, gesturing towards Athena's unconventional attire.

Before Athena could respond, a figure emerged from the shadows, aiming a gun directly at her. My heart lurched in my chest.

"Athena, watch out!" I roared, adrenaline coursing through me.

Just as the trigger was about to be pulled, an arrow materialized from nowhere, piercing the assassin's head in a clean shot.

A smug grin spread across Athena's face. "Backup courtesy of some friendly hunters," she announced. "Now let's get out of here. We have a tight schedule."

Urgency laced her voice as she grabbed my hand and we bolted out of the cell, the others hot on our heels.

"Slow down!" I yelled, struggling to keep pace with her frantic sprint.

"No time!" she countered over her shoulder. "The building's rigged to explode. The hunters have already freed the warriors."

The mention of bombs sent shivers down everyone's spine. We pushed ourselves further, fueled by the ticking clock of destruction. Finally, Athena skidded to a halt at what appeared to be the building's exit.

With a mighty kick, she shattered the door and barked orders. "Everyone out! We have thirty seconds!"

We scrambled through the doorway, joining a growing group already assembled outside. Just as we reached a safe distance behind the building, a colossal explosion ripped through the air, sending flames shooting skyward.

I instinctively wrapped my arms around Athena, pulling her close as she buried her head in my chest, overwhelmed by the sight of the inferno.

Turning back, we watched as the remaining flames licked at the skeletal remains of the building.

Suddenly, a slow clapping sound echoed through the clearing. All heads swiveled towards the source - Damon, emerging from the smoke with a battalion of rogues at his back.

"How many lives do you have, Athena?" he sneered, a twisted joy flickering in his eyes. "Is this getting tiresome? Perhaps this time, I'll ensure it's permanent."

"It's getting old, Damon," Athena retorted, her voice laced with steel. "Tired of your little games. I know you're bitter about losing your wolf, but just get it over with so I can end you!"

A twisted smile contorted his face. "Fine then, you want to finish this game? Let's finish it."

Rogues surged forward, their eyes gleaming with malice. My body screamed in protest, the wolfbane's aftereffects still lingering. Despite my weakness, I fought back with everything I had.

Chaos erupted as the two sides clashed. Suddenly, a vice grip clamped down on my arms, immobilizing me. Across the battlefield, Damon held Athena hostage, a cruel smile twisting his lips.

"Any last words, my love?" he taunted.

A growl rumbled deep within me.

Athena, her eyes gleaming with defiance, met his gaze head-on. "Talia!" With a bellow that cleaved through the battlefield's cacophony, she called out.

A whooshing sound filled the air as a band of cloaked figures descended from the trees - the hunters Athena mentioned earlier. With a defiant shove, she pushed Damon off her and sprinted towards me.

She punched the rogues holding me down and helped me up.

"Drink this." She handed me a glass vile.

"Why?" I asked.

"Just do it!" She commanded.

I gulped it down.

I got a slight headache but it vanished.

'Miss me.' Jordan's voice appeared in my head.

"What was that stuff?" I asked.

"Wolfsbane."

"What!?" My stare pierced into her like she'd just fed me poison, which, in all honesty, she had.

"Don't worry. I modified it to act as a strength booster."

I instantly relaxed.

"It's time to fight." She stated

As everyone started to kill each other.

CHAPTER TWENTY-EIGHT
~Athena~

"BETH!" My voice cut through the chaos as I bellowed her name. Her head whipped around, and without hesitation, I tossed a vial strapped to a similar glass container as Hayden's. "Distribute these to everyone who was locked up!" I barked the command, my gaze scanning the battlefield.

A curt nod was all she offered before she disappeared into the fray, dispensing the vials with practiced ease. The tide of battle had turned, our makeshift army clashing with Damon's rogues in a whirlwind of claws, fangs, and steel.

Suddenly, an arm snaked around my waist, the familiar warmth of Hayden grounding me momentarily. "Stay close, Athena," he rasped, his voice laced with worry. "Don't do anything reckless."

"Don't worry about me," I retorted, a confident smirk gracing my lips. With a well-practiced maneuver, I sidestepped the rogue's lunging attack. A flick of my wrist sent my sword singing through the air, finding its mark with a satisfying thud in the beast's chest. "See? I can handle myself just fine."

"Just stay by my side," he pleaded, his eyes scanning the battlefield with a fierce intensity.

With a sigh, I conceded. "Fine," I grumbled, "but you be careful too."

A quick peck on the lips was all the time I could spare before another rogue lunged towards me, meeting the sharp edge of my blade. A whistle pierced the air, drawing my attention to Grandpa tossing my bow and quivering with uncanny accuracy.

Strapping them on with practiced ease, I offered him a grateful smile, though I opted to stick with the familiar weight of the sword for now. A glance around revealed Justin and Beth wreaking havoc – Justin channeling crackling lightning through his fingertips, while Beth manipulated the very trees to ensnare her enemies.

"Athena!" Damon's voice echoed across the fight, dripping with a twisted joy, laced with a sickening amusement. "And here I thought you'd be lonely. But fear not, I've brought company!"

From the dense foliage emerged a figure I knew all too well – Beth's ex-mate, Alpha Mac, leading his entire pack. The sight instantly broke Beth's concentration, all the rogues she'd trapped springing free. Her eyes glazed over, her body stiffening into a lifeless statue of despair.

The vulnerable state didn't go unnoticed. We – Justin, Tyler, and I – formed a protective circle around her, fending off the opportunistic rogues aiming to exploit her weakness.

"Come on, mate," Alpha Mac's voice dripped with false sincerity. "You know you missed me."

Our heads snapped in his direction, Tyler letting out a low growl that sent shivers down my spine. Rage surged through me, hot and blistering. He had no right to her, no right to call her "mate" with such a possessive smirk.

"You're dead!" I screamed, my voice echoing over the clash of steel.

He whipped his head towards me, a snarl twisting his features. The familiar shift into his wolf form confirmed his fate. Before he could react, I lunged forward, the tip of my sword finding its mark – straight through his gaping maw and out his back.

"That's what you get for being a sorry excuse for an alpha," I spat, wrenching the blade free.

A bloodcurdling scream ripped from Beth's throat, her hands clutching her chest in a vice-like grip. The remaining wolves of Alpha Mac's pack whimpered, the alpha bond forcing them to share his excruciating pain.

Wasting no time, I rushed to Beth's side, injecting the vial into her arm. A jolt of energy coursed through her, her eyes snapping open with newfound clarity.

"What happened? Wait, I don't even want to know! I'm starving! Can I eat? No, never mind, we're in a battle... why did I feel pain? Did I...?" Her voice trailed off into a rapid mumble, thankfully cut short by Tyler silencing her with a passionate kiss.

In case you were wondering, yes, I gave her a much-needed sugar rush with my anti-wolfsbane serum.

Finally pulling away, Tyler scanned the battlefield. The tide had shifted decisively in our favor – most of Damon's and Alpha Mac's rogues were either incapacitated or fleeing for their lives.

"Beth," I said, my voice firm, "we'll talk later. But right now, I need you to tie Damon to that tree." I shook her gently, trying to break through her post-sugar-rush daze.

"Okay," she mumbled, her eyes regaining focus. "But I gotta get close, right?"

A low growl rumbled from Tyler's throat.

"Not that kind of close, you goof!" Beth retorted, rolling her eyes.

A sigh escaped my lips as I rolled my eyes. "Follow me," I instructed my voice firm despite the chaos around us. Rogues charged towards us, desperate to impede our progress towards Damon. Each lunge was met with a practiced flick of my wrist, the sword a deadly blur as it dispatched one foe after another. We were mere yards from Damon, victory almost within our grasp.

"Beth, tie him to that tree now!" I barked the command, urgency lacing my tone. A curt nod was her only response as she manipulated the nearby tree, its branches wrapping around Damon like a living cage. Confusion clouded his features, followed by a surge of frantic struggle. His eyes met mine, a desperate plea flickering within them as Beth tightened her hold. A pained groan escaped his lips.

With a determined glint in my eyes, I charged towards him, the weight of the sword a familiar comfort in my hand. The world seemed to hold its breath, both sides of the battle locked in a stunned silence as all eyes fixated on me. Damon continued to struggle, fear momentarily replacing his usual arrogance, though he quickly masked it with a determined scowl.

I stopped just a hair's breadth away from him, the tip of the blade hovering ominously over his chest. "This time, I'll make sure you stay dead," I growled, my voice laced with a deadly promise.

Just as I was about to deliver the final blow, a sound shattered the tense silence – a child's innocent laughter. My head snapped towards the source, the sword frozen in mid-air. A small girl, no older than three, emerged from the treeline, her eyes wide with curiosity. A flicker of surprise crossed Damon's face before a smile tugged at the corners of his lips.

"Avery," he scolded gently, "I told you not to follow me."

The little girl, her name apparently Avery, pouted momentarily before flashing a disarming smile. "Sorry Daddy, I was just bored," she pouted, her eyes darting between us in confusion. "Daddy, why are you with a superhero and a tree?"

Damon chuckled, his voice strained. "Just playing with some friends, sweetheart."

His words sent a jolt through me. "You have a kid?" I blurted, disbelief coloring my voice.

Before I could get a response from Damon, Avery shook her head. "He's not my actual daddy," she clarified. "My mommy and daddy got stuck in their car and became stars in the sky. He found me and helped me."

A smug smirk played on Damon's lips as he turned towards me. "See, Athena? Fate has a way of keeping me alive."

I met his gaze unflinchingly. "I've told you, Damon, I don't believe in fate. Fate doesn't dictate my actions," I declared, severing the tree's grasp with a resolute swing. "This is my choice. You live... for the girl's sake."

"Consider this a reprieve, Robin Hood," Damon replied, a hint of amusement in his voice. He took Avery's hand, and together they disappeared into the forest depths.

A strong grip circled my wrist, spinning me around to face a bewildered Hayden. "Why did you let him go?" he demanded, his voice tight with concern.

"The little girl," I explained. "Sure, Damon's a bad guy, but he clearly cares about her. He wouldn't put her in danger."

"What makes you think that?" he countered, his brow furrowed.

"I know Damon better than you think," I insisted, the truth hanging heavy in the air. "He won't hurt her."

Hayden, ever the pragmatist, sighed in resignation. "I respect your decision." He leaned in, his lips brushing against mine in a comforting kiss. "The rogues are neutralized. We can finally go home."

Relief washed over me as I took his hand, a wave of exhaustion threatening to pull me under. Thankfully, no casualties had been suffered on our side, though injuries were plentiful. A glance down at Hayden revealed a bloodstain spreading across his shirt. My concern flared, and I reached out to inspect the wound.

"You should have told me you were hurt," I scolded, my voice laced with worry.

"It's already healed," he dismissed my concern with a nonchalant shrug.

I rolled my eyes, frustration momentarily eclipsing my relief. Just then, a faint voice echoed in my head.

'Jean?' I questioned internally.

'Yeah,' came the reply, barely a whisper.

'Did I do the right thing?' I asked, the weight of my decision pressing down on me.

'Of course, you did,' Jean soothed. 'Avery would have been alone.

'Then why do I feel-' my thoughts were interrupted by Hayden.

"Athena?"

"Hm." I looked up at him.

"Are you ok?" He asked.

I nodded slowly. "Yeah, I'm fine."

He nodded and kept walking.

'Jean if I did the right thing, then why do I feel like I made a mistake.'

'Don't worry about it. You know we have bigger things to worry about.' She reminded me.

With a hand on my belly, I whispered, "I know, Jean. I know."

CHAPTER TWENTY-NINE

~Athena~

"Where is she!?" I heard a familiar voice scream.

I walked out of the closet and was met with an angry and worried Hayden.

His worried expression softened the moment he saw me. He reached out, pulling me close in a warm hug.

He gripped me tighter, his voice firm. "You aren't going anywhere."

A playful smile tugged at my lips. "What about bathroom breaks?"

His eyes held a teasing glint. "Five minutes, tops. Any longer than that, and I'm coming in to get you."

"What if I just want to be alone?"

"Then you'll be alone with me."

"You're being dramatic."

"No, I'm not!" He said in a whiney voice.

I looked at him weirdly. "And sensitive."

He glared at me and then picked me up bridal style. They threw me on the bed which resulted in me bouncing. He caught me before I fell off the bed.

"Don't do that!" I yelled slightly.

He looked at me confused as he hovered above me.

I buried my face in my hands. "I'm sorry."

His grip tore my hands from my face, pinning them mercilessly above my head.

"What's bothering you? You've been more moody than usual." He asked.

'Athena, it's time to tell him.' Jean popped up in my head but was barely audible.

'I'm worried. What if he doesn't want it to happen.'

'Then he deals with it. With us or not.' She disappeared from my head.

I removed my hands from Hayden's grip and made him sit down in front of me.

My voice barely a whisper, I managed, "I have something important to tell you."

My hormones kicked in and I started crying.

Hayden cupped my face with both hands and wiped my tears with his thumbs. "Hey, don't cry. We can handle anything."

"Hayden I'm…" The door opened cutting me off and revealing Xavier.

"Are you PMS'ing?" He asked me.

I flipped him off and ignored his glare.

"What do you want Xavier?" Hayden asked Xavier in the mindlink.

"All the warriors and the hunters that were injured are at the hospital. Luckily no one died." He explained.

"Anything else?" Hayden asked.

"Summer just had a doctor's appointment and her baby's coming in three weeks! Her emotions are a rollercoaster, and I need some serious backup."

"How about we let her hold one of Midnight's puppies to calm her down?" I suggested.

"Oh so she's allowed to hold a puppy but I'm not allowed to teach them to skateboard. That's low."

I rolled my eyes at him. "Just go take care of your mate."

He rolled his eyes and closed the door as he left.

Hayden turned to me and kissed my forehead. "Tell me what's bothering you."

I looked down at my lap and then back at him. "I'm pregnant."

All the color drained from his face and he stayed silent.

"I knew it. You don't want it." I choked out, tears streaming down my face. I bolted for the nearest guest room, slamming the door behind me.

I locked the door and slid my back down on the door.

I could feel Jean whimpering silently but she was focused on protecting our baby.

I crawled on the bed and cried myself to sleep.

~Hayden~

Athena ran out of the room crying.

'You little shit! Why did you do that!?' Jordan growled at me.

'I didn't mean to! I was just shocked.'

'And you couldn't kiss her or hug her to tell her that we do want it!'

'I was still processing what she said!'

'She's carrying our child! What's there to process!?'

'You're right I've been a little shit, but now she won't want to see me.'

'Go to her before I do!' He growled.

I went to the guest room that Athena ran to.

I knocked on the door softly.

"Athena?" I called out.
No reply.
"Athena let me in."
Silence.
"I'm coming in."
I turned the nob but the door was locked.
"Always stubborn and difficult," I mumbled to myself.
I kicked down the door.
Athena was asleep on the bed. Her face was tear-stained and her eyes and nose were red and puffy.
I picked her up bridal style and walked back to our room. I laid her down on our bed and placed a kiss on her stomach.
Midnight came in with a few of her puppies and they all laid down next to Athena's stomach.
I sat down next to Athena and shook her awake.
She stirred around in her sleep. When she opened her eyes I slammed my lips onto hers.
She gasped but quickly recovered and kissed back. I'm pretty sure she didn't want to but she did it anyway.
I pulled away.
"You can't just kiss me and expect me not to be mad at you." She pointed out.
"I want this child. I don't want you to think that I don't want it." I went straight to the point.
"Is that you talking or Jordan?" She narrowed her eyes.
"Don't look at me like that! Of course, it's me."
"Then why didn't you say anything!?"

"Because I'm worried. I worried that I might not be the perfect dad. Worried that I might disappoint you."

"You don't have to be perfect. You just have to be there for our child." She placed a hand on the side of my face.

I brought her lips to mine.

"You can never disappoint me." She mumbled against my lips.

"I hope you're right."

Lifting her shirt slightly, I placed a kiss on her exposed stomach. "Hey there, little one," I spoke softly. "You're destined to be a powerful Alpha, regardless of whether you're a boy or a girl. I'll love you unconditionally."

As I released her shirt, a radiant smile bloomed on Athena' face.

"And I love you," I breathed, my voice thick with emotion.

Wrapping her arms around my neck, she pulled me into a tight embrace. "I love you too," she whispered, her voice barely audible.

Her lips met mine in a passionate kiss, then she playfully tugged on my lower lip. A groan escaped me as I leaned in for another kiss, but she playfully denied me access.

Pulling away, I feigned disappointment. "Even after all this, you still manage to tease me,"

A mischievous glint sparkled in her eyes. "Maybe I do," she purred. "Want to see just how much of a tease I can be?"

With a playful bark, Midnight and her pups scampered out of the room. Locking the door behind them, a single thought echoed in my mind: "Maybe I do."

CHAPTER THIRTY

~Athena~

I stirred awake, the soft cotton of one of Hayden's oversized shirts clinging to my body. He lay beside me, fast asleep, his arm possessively wrapped around my waist.

Tentatively, I tried to slip free from his hold, but he stirred and tightened his grip.

"Don't leave," he mumbled, his voice thick with sleep as he nuzzled his face into the crook of my neck.

"It's been a week, Hayden," I pointed out. "I understand your concern, but I don't need that level of protection right now."

A week since I'd told him about the baby.

He mumbled something incoherent against my skin. "I don't care. You're not going anywhere. Especially now."

"Just let me get my day started, please?" I pleaded.

A mischievous grin seemed to radiate from him. "No meetings today, so you don't have to rush."

"But I want to check on Summer," I persisted. "She has a doctor's appointment today, and I promised I'd go with her."

His face fell into a pout. "Fine. But you're showering with me first."

He peeled himself off the bed and padded towards the bathroom, clad only in his boxers. With a raised eyebrow, I sat up and watched him go.

"Coming or not?" he called back, the amusement evident in his voice.

The sound of the shower filled the room as I rose from the bed.

••••

~Xavier~

"Ooh, bacon!" I declared, reaching for a crispy strip. But before I could grab it, Summer swatted my hand away with a spatula.

"Hey!" I whined, rubbing my sore hand.

'Such a drama king,' Jack, my wolf, snarked in my head.

'Thanks for the support, buddy,' I retorted sarcastically.

Summer pulled me back to reality. "That bacon is mine."

"Only because you're carrying a little one," I conceded, planting a quick kiss on her lips.

"Don't touch me!" she snapped.

Her mood swings were giving me whiplash! Yesterday, she was all over me, and now she couldn't stand the thought of me being near her.

"Okay, okay, sorry," I mumbled, leaning against the counter, my mind going a mile a minute.

A barrage of random thoughts filled my head:

Why do janitors whistle while they clean? Do they enjoy their jobs?

Why suits for secret agents? Sweatpants would be way more comfortable and practical for all that sneaking around.

If my wolf is considered 'my' wolf, does that technically make me human?

Will food ever taste even better?

Why can't kids stay inside the coloring lines? They're there for a reason!

The word "impatient" actually spells "I'm patient" backward.

"Xavier!" A jolt from Summer's voice yanked me back to reality.

"What's wrong?" I asked, panic starting to rise.

A small puddle was spreading on the floor next to her leg.

"What do you think?!" she yelled. "My water broke!"

My eyes widened in shock. Scooping her up bridal style, I sprinted for the car.

Reaching the vehicle, I gently placed her in the passenger seat and peeled out of the driveway, speeding towards the hospital like a bat out of hell.

"I'm two weeks early! Get this baby out of me!" she screamed, her voice tight with pain.

"Don't worry, babe, we're almost there," I reassured her, adrenaline coursing through my veins.

The hospital came into view, and I practically threw the car into the park. Grabbing Summer in my arms again, I kicked open the emergency room doors.

"She's going into labor! Help!" I bellowed, drawing the attention of the entire medical staff.

Doctors and nurses rushed towards us in a flurry of white coats. I carefully transferred Summer to a gurney as they whisked her away into one of the emergency rooms.

Following them, I watched as they hooked her up to machines and cut her pants off. A female doctor entered the room with a determined look on her face. "Alright, Summer, I need you to push," she instructed.

••••

The nurse entered, cradling a tiny bundle in a soft pink blanket. "Xavier, Summer, meet your beautiful baby girl!" she announced.

Summer's face lit up as the nurse placed the baby in her arms. "What do you think about Elsa?" Summer asked, her voice filled with hope.

"Perfect," I replied, leaning in to plant a kiss on Summer's forehead. We both gazed in awe at our daughter, Elsa, who blinked open her bright blue eyes that mirrored Summer's.

"She's your twin," I commented.

Just as Summer was about to reply, the door burst open with a bang. "Move it! Where's my niece?" Athena barged in, bumping me aside with her hip. Little Elsa responded with a burst of giggles.

"Looks like she already finds you hilarious," Athena smirked.

"Guess she gets her funny bone from me then," I retorted, regaining my balance.

Athena rolled her eyes playfully. "Hey there, cutie pie," she cooed to the baby.

Hayden followed Athena in. "Thanks," he muttered, earning a playful glare from Athena for mistaking her greeting.

I scooped up Elsa, savoring the moment. "If she inherits even a fraction of your chaotic energy, she'll need all the luck she can get," Athena teased.

Summer chuckled. "Way to ruin the sweet moment."

Jamie and Robert arrived, their faces beaming with excitement. "How did everything go?" Jamie inquired.

"Everything went smoothly," Summer replied. "She came a little early, but the doctors said she'll be just fine."

"Let me hold her!" Athena demanded, extending her arms.

I playfully cautioned her, "Just be careful, okay?"

Athena playfully rolled her eyes again. Elsa cooed and giggled as Athena gently touched her nose.

"See, she likes me more," Athena declared with a smug grin.

I playfully crossed my arms and mumbled, "Sure she does."

Elsa's giggles intensified at my reaction, melting my mock frown into a genuine smile.

Athena carefully passed Elsa to Hayden. Elsa playfully swatted at Hayden's face with her tiny hand.

"Looks like a warrior in the making," Hayden mused. "Third in command might need to watch out."

"No! No way am I letting her anywhere near danger!" I protested.

Elsa's happy expression faltered, replaced by a whimper. My resolve crumbled instantly. "Alright, alright," I conceded, "maybe she can be a warrior."

Relieved by the change in tone, Elsa's tears vanished, replaced by a happy gurgle.

"She already has you wrapped around her tiny finger," Summer observed with amusement.

Jamie took a turn holding Elsa, tickling her tummy and teasing me playfully. Robert, ever the calm one, simply held her gently and spoke in soothing tones.

Finally, Elsa was back in my arms. She reached out, her tiny hand landing on my nose.

"What's her name?" Athena asked.

"Elsa," Summer informed her.

"Elsa, that's lovely. A perfect name for a future Gamma," Robert said with a smile.

Laughter filled the room as we all imagined our daughter's future adventures.

As yawns escaped both Elsa and Summer, Jamie announced, "We'll let you two get some rest."

One by one, our friends and family filed out, leaving us alone with our precious newborn. I gently placed Elsa in the crib, watching as she drifted off to sleep with a peaceful sigh.

Summer shifted slightly in the bed, making space for me. I climbed in beside her and pulled her close. "I love you," I whispered.

"I love you too," she murmured, snuggling closer. "Get some sleep. I know you'll want to be well-rested for our little warrior."

I nodded, a smile playing on my lips. Summer drifted off to sleep, muttering something in her sleep about our "little warrior." And as I looked at my beautiful family, I couldn't agree more. Today, our world has changed forever, and I wouldn't have it any other way.

EPILOGUE
~One month later~
~Athena~

"Hayden! Bring me ice cream!" I bellowed from the living room.

"On my way!" Hayden's reply echoed from the kitchen, laced with a hint of exasperation even though he tried to sound calm.

He emerged with a tub of cookies 'and cream and a spoon, a playful glint in his eyes despite his pretended annoyance.

I snatched the tub from him and dug right in. "No 'thank you'?" Hayden teased, settling down beside me on the couch.

"Mmm, right," I mumbled between bites, turning my attention back to the ice cream. "Thank you, ice cream, for being so darn delicious."

Hayden pouted playfully. "You, woman, are lucky I love you."

"Oh please," I countered with a smirk, "you're the lucky one for getting this ice cream to me before the craving monster took over."

It had been a month, and my stomach already resembled a basketball. Elsa, too, seemed to be growing in leaps and bounds, looking more like a six-month-old than a one-month-old already.

Jean remained distant, consumed by her protective instincts towards our little one. The baby's gender was still a mystery, a shared decision fueled by the thrill of the unknown.

"Speaking of surprises," Hayden announced, changing the subject, "I have one planned for you later today."

My eyes lit up. "Chocolate?" I shot hopefully.

"Nope."

"Ice cream?"

"Not even ice cream, love."

The rapid-fire guesses continued – chocolate milk, any kind of food – all met with Hayden's teasing denials.

"Fine, then," I huffed playfully, digging another spoonful of ice cream. "Surprise or not, it's cutting into my ice cream time."

He leaned in, placing a quick kiss on my cheek. "Trust me, you'll love it."

"Well, it better be good," I mumbled, a playful glint in my eyes. "Every second counts when it comes to ice cream cravings."

He chuckled, then leaned in again, this time for a lingering kiss. A playful swipe of his tongue sent a shiver down my spine.

"Hey!" I exclaimed playfully, swatting at his arm. "Was that to get the ice cream off my face?"

A mischievous grin spread across his face. "Maybe," he admitted.

I couldn't help but smirk, finishing off the ice cream with a satisfied sigh.

••••

The anticipation was killing me. "There yet?" With a playful lilt in my voice, I whined, my impatience barely disguised by the teasing tone.

Hayden chuckled, the sound rumbling in my chest from beside me. "Almost, love."

He'd blindfolded me for the drive, and the lack of sight only fueled my curiosity. What could he possibly have planned? A fancy restaurant? A weekend getaway? My mind raced with possibilities as the car rumbled along.

Finally, the engine sputtered to a stop. A door creaked open, then slammed shut. I fumbled with the handle on my side, but a strong hand clamped over mine before I could open it.

"Careful," Hayden cautioned, his voice laced with amusement. "Gotta get you there in one piece for the surprise"

I couldn't help but roll my eyes, even though he couldn't see me. This playful protectiveness of his was endearing, even as it made me feel a little clumsy. He helped me out, his hand warm and steady beneath mine.

A moment of silence followed, and then Hayden gently removed the blindfold. The world blinked into focus, and I gasped.

There, nestled amidst rolling green hills, stood a house. A beautiful, sprawling house, bathed in the warm glow of the setting sun. It radiated warmth and welcome, its windows like friendly eyes winking at me.

"Hayden?" I whispered, my voice thick with emotion. This wasn't just a house, it was a dream come true. A place for our child to grow up, a place for our family to run wild with Midnight and her pups. A place to build a future together.

A slow smile spread across Hayden's face. "Our home, love," he announced, his voice filled with pride. "A place to raise our children, watch the pups chase butterflies, and create a lifetime of memories."

Tears welled up in my eyes. This wasn't just a surprise, it was a symbol of everything we'd built together – our love, our struggles, our hopes for the future. But before I could voice my gratitude, a sharp pain lanced through my abdomen. I gasped, clutching my breath.

"My water broke," I managed to blurt out, my voice shaky.

In an instant, Hayden's playful demeanor vanished. His eyes widened with concern, a fierce protectiveness replacing the amusement. With practiced ease, he scooped me into his arms and rushed me back to the car.

The drive to the hospital was a blur. The world outside became a cacophony of flashing lights and rushing sounds. Hayden weaved through traffic, his voice a low growl that seemed to command the road to yield. He wouldn't let anything stop us from reaching that hospital, from reaching the future we were about to welcome.

Pain tore through me with every bump in the road, every twist and turn. I clung to Hayden, drawing strength from his unwavering presence. His hand squeezed mine, his alpha strength a silent promise.

The hospital doors burst open, a primal cry echoing through the sterile halls. I didn't care about protocol then, didn't care about the stares or the hushed whispers. All that mattered was the love radiating from Hayden and the life pulsing within me.

"Help her!" Hayden roared his voice a force of nature.

Doctors rushed in, their white coats a stark contrast to the raw emotions on display. As they whisked me away, my eyes locked with Hayden's. A silent promise passed between us. He would be there for me, every step of the way.

••••

The new moon hung heavy in the sky, a silent witness to the end of one chapter and the thrilling beginning of another. Athena, exhausted but exhilarated, cradled a tiny bundle in her arms – a healthy baby girl, with eyes the color of twilight. Her name whispered in the air, filled the room with warmth – Amanda, daughter of the Alpha and the Huntress, a howl under a new moon.

THE END

ABOUT THE AUTHOR

Dive into the mystical realms of paranormal romance with bestselling author Emma Roberts. Emma Roberts isn't your typical romance writer. Don't get her wrong, she swoons over grand gestures and happily-ever-afters as much as the next hopeless romantic. But her stories are born from a different kind of love – the love for the fantastical, the thrill of a world where wolves transform and destinies intertwine.

Emma spent her childhood nose-deep in fantasy novels, escaping into worlds where anything was possible. She dreamed of strong heroines and brooding heroes, of soul-deep connections that defied all odds. When she wasn't lost in a book, she was crafting her fantastical tales, filling notebooks with stories of mythical creatures and epic love stories.

"The Huntress Forbidden Mate" is a culmination of that childhood passion. It's a story that whispers of second chances, of finding love in the most unexpected places. Emma weaves a world where rejection stings but doesn't break, where determination and a fierce belief in love can overcome any obstacle.

More than just a love story, "The Huntress Forbidden Mate" is a celebration of female strength and the power of vulnerability. It's a story Emma poured her heart into, a testament to the enduring power of love and the magic that blooms when we embrace our true selves.

So, if you're looking for an escape filled with heart-pounding moments, heartwarming characters, and a love story that will leave you breathless, then Emma invites you to step into the world of "The Huntress Forbidden Mate" .Prepare to be swept away by a love that defies tradition and a happily-ever-after you won't soon forget.

AUTHOR'S NOTE

Dear Reader,

Did "The Huntress Forbidden Mate" by Emma Roberts whisk you away on a moonlit adventure? Did you lose yourself in its enchanting world, heart pounding with the thrill of the hunt and the mystery of the unknown?

As the author, your thoughts are like whispered secrets from a loyal pack mate. They hold immense value, guiding others who yearn to follow the trail I has blazed.

Did the moonlight dance on your skin as you explored the alluring world of ? Did you find yourself swept away by the characters' destinies, their loves, their losses? Did the twists and turns leave you breathless, eager to see what awaited around the next bend?.

Sharing your experience on Goodreads, Amazon, or any platform you call home is a gift. It's a flickering torch illuminating the path for others considering this journey. Your honest words empowers me to weave even more captivating tales that resonate with kindred spirits like you.

Thank you for joining me on this quest. Your reflections on "The Huntress forbidden mate" are eagerly awaited, as they are the very essence of an author's growth.

With heartfelt gratitude,

Emma Roberts

ADDITIONAL RESOURCES

Dear Reader,

It brings me immense joy to reconnect with you once more.

I extend my heartfelt gratitude for your steadfast support and interest in "The Huntress Forbidden Mate" by Emma Roberts. If you found this tale of paranormal romance captivating and are yearning for more immersive experiences, allow me to recommend some of my other works that may pique your interest:

For a journey through otherworldly realms and enthralling adventures, I invite you to explore my Author Central page on Amazon. There, you'll discover a diverse array of novels and stories crafted with the same passion and imagination that brought "The Huntress Forbidden Mate" to life.

Feel free to scan the QR code on the next page or simply click the link to access my Author Central page:

https://www.amazon.com/author/emmarobertsromancenovels

Your continued support means everything to me, and I remain committed to providing you with tales that inspire and captivate. Thank you for being an integral part of this literary journey, and may my stories continue to bring you joy and wonder.
Warm regards,
Emma Roberts